As Long As There Are Mountains

BOOKS BY NATALIE KINSEY-WARNOCK

THE BEAR THAT HEARD CRYING
THE CANADA GEESE QUILT
THE FIDDLER OF THE NORTHERN LIGHTS
THE NIGHT THE BELLS RANG
SWEET MEMORIES STILL
WHEN SPRING COMES
THE WILD HORSES OF SWEETBRIAR
WILDERNESS CAT

As Long As There Are Mountains

Natalie Kinsey-Warnock

Cobblehill Books/Dutton
New York

To Shirley

with love, gratitude for her friendship,

and admiration for her strength

and courage

Library of Congress Cataloging-in-Publication Data
Kinsey-Warnock, Natalie.
As long as there are mountains / Natalie Kinsey-Warnock.
p.   cm.
Summary: Thirteen-year-old Iris dreams of one day running the
family farm in northern Vermont, but the summer of 1956 hold
many shocking changes that threaten the life Iris loves.
ISBN 0-525-65236-1
[1. Farm life—Vermont—Fiction.   2. Family life—Fiction.
3. Conduct of life—Fiction.]   I. Title.
PZ7.K6293As 1997
[Fic]—dc21   96-48531   CIP   AC

Published in the United States by Cobblehill Books,
an affiliate of Dutton Children's Books,
a division of Penguin Books USA Inc.,
375 Hudson Street, New York, New York 10014
Designed by Charlotte Staub
Printed in the United States of America   First Edition
10 9 8 7 6 5 4 3 2 1

PROLOGUE

Once, on a hot June afternoon, when I was nine years old, my mother sent me out to the fields with a jug of ginger water for my father. He and my brother were haying, Father mowing and Lucien raking, and Mama knew they'd be thirsty. The air rang with the *clack-clack* of the cutter bars and I remember yellow butterflies fluttered up as I strode through the grass, the jug swinging cold against my leg.

They both stopped for a drink and it struck me for the first time how much alike they looked, arms and faces brown from the sun, their shirts dark with sweat. They were standing close, and Father rested his hand on Lucien's shoulder. I remember that particularly because my father was not a man who hugged or kissed his children, but the dry weather had put him in a good mood.

"You know," Father said, his eyes roaming the fields and green hills beyond. "Someday, this will all be yours," and he climbed on his tractor and mowed away, leaving Lucien and me in his wake. Anyone watching us would have seen anger, or at least disappointment, on both our faces, Lucien because he knew he didn't want the farm, and me because I did. And the thought that's been on my mind since then, almost four years now from that hot June afternoon, is: why couldn't Father have said that to me?

CHAPTER ONE

I peeled long strips of bark from the cedar post and set the post in the hole Father had made with the iron bar. Father raised the post maul over his head and brought it down BAM!, driving the post deep into the ground.

Father wiped the sweat from his forehead and looked over his shoulder. Behind us, a row of new posts stretched to the other side of the pasture. They gleamed yellow in the warm spring sunshine.

"That's a good morning's work," Father said. "If we didn't have to go to that dadblame wedding this afternoon, we could finish up this fence," and that's when I knew Father didn't want to go to my cousin Aletta's wedding anymore than I did.

"Let's just stay here then," I said. Fence-building wasn't one of my favorite things but it was better than going to a dumb wedding. And I enjoyed the feeling that Father needed me. Ever since Lucien had gone off to college in the fall, I'd been helping Father with all the work around the farm.

But Father shook his head.

"Your mother would skin us both," he said.

A car horn honked and we looked toward the road. A large man I didn't know stood next to a car I didn't recognize, a big fancy car. The man was dressed up in a suit and he gestured wildly for us to walk over to him.

"I don't see anything wrong with *his* legs, do you?" Father asked me, and I giggled.

As we approached, I noticed the car had New York plates. What was a New York car doing way out here?

"I was driving by and couldn't help admiring what a beautiful place you have here," the man said. "My wife and I are looking to move to the country when I retire next year. Might we be able to talk you into selling this place?"

"Nope," Father said, and turned to get back to his fence-building.

"Wait one moment," the man said, reaching into his pocket. He handed Father a business card. "Here's my name and number, in case you change your mind."

"I won't," Father said.

I had to run to keep up with him as he strode back to the fenceline.

"Father, you wouldn't sell the farm, would you?" I asked.

"You just heard me tell him no," Father said.

"I mean ever."

"Well, Iris," said Father, "ever's a long time, and we don't know what will happen in the future. But don't you worry about it." That didn't ease my mind at all. In my experience, whenever grown-ups say not to worry that means something's going on they don't want you to know.

My father was a happy man, generally speaking. People commented on his laugh and smile. But lately he'd seemed worried and I suspected there was money trouble. I'd seen him and Mama poring over the account books, talking in hushed whispers, and Father had had two meetings with the bank president. I guess I hadn't let it worry me too much (which was a wonder since Mama calls me a worry-wart) because that's the way farming is. There's always more money going out: paying for seed and fertilizer and grain and new machinery or parts for old machinery you're trying to nurse along, than there is money coming in. And just when you think there might be a profit this year, some disaster happens, like too much rain, or not enough rain, or gale winds blow your barn roof off, or lightning kills some of your cows, and you're in debt again. Father tells a joke about a farmer who wins a million dollars. Folks ask him what he's gonna do with it and the farmer says, "Well, I guess I'll just keep farming till it's all gone," and I'd say that just about sums up farming, economically speaking.

But people don't go into farming for the money. It's other things that hold us close to the land: growing and harvesting our own food that we've sweated over and worried about, feeling the rhythms of the seasons in our blood, holding earth in our hands and knowing by the feel of it when it's time to plant, taking care of land that our parents and grandparents lived on and worked and handed down to us to care for till we pass it on.

Helping Father the past winter, there'd been mornings I'd hated it. Stumbling out of bed in the dark and cold to feed twenty-six calves, then having to wash the barn smell off me before school. I didn't want the kids to laugh at me like they did at Norman Riley who always reeked of manure and silage like he'd rolled in them.

"You know," Father said, breaking into my thoughts. "I guess it won't be too long before I'll be going to your wedding."

Father might as well have hit me with the post maul.

"I'm never getting married," I answered hotly. "I'm going to live here forever."

Father just smiled and pounded in another post.

We heard a shout and watched Ferris March, my best friend, pedal along the cowpath, her bike bouncing over the ruts.

"A regular parade of people coming by here today," Father said wryly.

"Where're you headed?" I called out to Ferris.

"Mom sent me to get some dandelion greens for supper," she called back. "Can you come along?"

I looked at Father, but I knew the answer. To Father, work always came before play and we weren't finished with the fence yet. But Father surprised me.

"Oh, go on," he said. "You've got a couple of hours before the wedding. I bet the fiddleheads are ready up on the hill, too. Pick a bag of those and we'll have them for your birthday supper tonight."

I sneaked a paper bag out of the house and hoped I'd get away without being seen, but Mama's like a bloodhound that way, always picking up on things you're trying to keep hidden.

"Just where do you think you're going, young lady?" she said. My heart sank.

"Ferris and I are going to get dandelion greens and fiddleheads."

"You're not heading out this close to the wedding," Mama said.

"Father said I could," I protested. Mama says arguing with her is one of my favorite pastimes. "He said for me to bring some fiddleheads for my birthday supper."

I could practically see the wheels turn in Mama's head while she decided. I think it was me mentioning my birthday that clinched it. She looked at the clock.

"You have two hours," she said. "You just make sure you're back by one o'clock. I'll have your clothes ready for you."

I glared at her as I went out, slamming the screen door behind me. Maybe I wouldn't be back by one o'clock. I was still mad at her for what she'd told me last night.

Before bed, Mama had set me down and said it was time I started acting more ladylike, meaning, among other things, that I'd have to dress up for the wedding. I had to start wearing a bra. And nylon stockings.

"Aunt Lurdine sent you over a brand new pair and suggested you wear them tomorrow for the wedding. She said they'd cover up the scabs on your knees."

I thought my air was being cut off. I treasured my freedom and my toughness. I was faster and stronger than any of the boys in my class and they respected me. ("Most of them fear you," Mama had said. "I should have made you act more like a lady a long time ago.") I was the only girl on their baseball team. If those boys saw the slightest weakness in me now, they'd start laughing at me and might kick me off the team. What business was it of Aunt Lurdine's, anyway?

I didn't like being a girl much, and I guess I'd always dreaded growing up. I'd tried not to think about it, but now, having Mama hit me with it right on, it made me kind of queasy. I pictured a wild horse being caught, bridled and saddled for the first time, always hating the feel of leather, forever thinking of the open plains and singing wind. Was it worse never to have known freedom than to lose it and always long for it? Aunt Lurdine would have said I was being melodramatic.

I hated Aunt Lurdine. Even her name, Lurdine. Then she'd married Sturgis Shoop to become Lurdine Shoop. Most people I would have felt sorry for, them having a name like that, but not Aunt Lurdine. She was loud and bossy, and I knew she didn't like me much, either. She intimidated my mother, too. My mother always acted unsure around her, and Mama could never say no to Aunt Lurdine's advice. Aunt Lurdine even lorded it over us how Sturgis had moved up in the company till now he was part owner, how ambitious he was and how he never would have been content to be a farmer. Father didn't let her bother him, but whenever she talked like that, Mama's mouth would get thin and pinched and she'd get real quiet.

I hated Aunt Lurdine for making Mama feel like she ought to shrink into herself. But for all her bragging about him, I don't think Aunt Lurdine liked Uncle Sturgis much. She never talked to him nice, barked orders at him like a drill sergeant, and kept telling him how lucky he was that she picked him to marry. Seemed like bad luck to me.

He had a funny name, Sturgis Shoop, but I liked Uncle Sturgis all right, and I felt sorry for him. He never acted uppity around us and he always had root beer barrels in his pocket for me. He worked in a furniture factory and always smelled of wood shavings and varnish. He didn't seem so ambitious to me. Henpecked, Father would say before Mama shushed him.

As Ferris and I climbed through the woods, sunlight filtered through the new leaves, pale as lettuce, and dappled the wildflowers beginning to blossom. I knelt among the red trillium and Dutchman's-breeches. I dug down into the dark, loamy soil and pulled up new leeks, shiny and white as bits of bone. We'd have them for supper, too; I liked them with vinegar and salt. Mama had once remarked to Father, "Pour vinegar on it and that girl would eat a shoe."

I put the leeks in my bag, along with the greens, and Ferris and I followed the cowpath out of the woods and into the high pasture on Beech Hill.

I loved the pasture. You couldn't see our house or barn from up here; you couldn't see any houses from here. This hill held more wildness than any place I knew, and I felt I belonged here. I could almost believe I was the first person to discover this hill, an explorer like Samuel de Champlain. A wind always blew up here, crossing the valley as it came straight from the ridge of the Green Mountains some thirty miles away, and I could feel it drawing the anger from me. Up here, nobody owned me.

"What do you think you're getting for your birthday?" Ferris asked.

I thought about Father's meetings at the bank and shrugged. I didn't expect much in the way of presents.

I breathed in deeply. The wind had picked up and brought us the smell of lilacs.

"I love lilacs, don't you?"

"Sure," said Ferris. "Doesn't everyone?"

"No," I said. "Not everyone."

Ferris tossed her head.

"Never knew anyone who didn't like lilacs," she said. But I had.

My grandfather had hated lilacs. When Grandpa was

eleven, his father had come home from a log drive with a pain in his belly and died three days later from a burst appendix, when the lilacs were in bloom and folks were planting great bouquets of them on gravestones for Decoration Day. To Grandpa, lilacs smelled of death.

But here on the hill, the wind also carried the delicate perfume of apple blossoms. Tomorrow I'd carry an armful to lay on Grandpa's grave. He had liked apple blossoms.

I'd worked so hard during the past few months to stop thinking of Grandpa all the time and then a smell had brought him instantly to mind. I still had nightmares about Grandpa. It had been almost a year since he'd died. I knew the date was etched in my mind forever, as surely as it was carved on his gravestone: May 18, 1955. Grandpa had been plowing on a steep field and the tractor had rolled over, crushing the life from him. Father had found him two hours later when Grandpa hadn't come home at noon for dinner. Only a year ago, but already there were days when I couldn't remember exactly what his face looked like. It scared me that I could forget so easily, but I could still smell the mustiness of the butternuts we cracked on cold winter nights, or feel his hands, as deeply ridged as the butternuts themselves. It was Grandpa who first taught me it was going to rain when the shriek of the train whistle could be heard from Orleans, twenty miles away, and showed me just where to look for the first tender morel mushrooms in the sugar bush below the barn.

There was so much up here on this hill to remind me of Grandpa and not far from where I sat was the cellar-hole of the house my great-great-grandfather Owen Campbell had built, when he came over from Scotland. Wild raspberries grew there now, but you could still find the granite stones that marked where the house had stood.

One look at the sun told me it was time I ought to be heading back. My stomach lurched. Why did this have to be happening? Why couldn't I just go on being who I was, and spend the rest of my life right here in the woods, living off the land?

I walked back, skirting the shoreline of the pond. The first swollen shoots of arum and arrowhead had pushed up through the dark mud, and the yellow blossoms of cowslips gleamed as brightly as bits of sunshine. Soon the wild blue iris would bloom. They were Mama's favorite flower and she'd fill pitchers with them to set on the table and piano.

I loved the wild iris, too: they made me think of bluebirds perched in the grass. But I didn't like my name. It seemed better suited for an eighty-year-old woman with a cane and an ear horn. I wanted to trade names with Ferris. I would have liked a Scottish name, to reflect my heritage, and Ferris was the Celtic form of Peter, though a much better name than Peter, I thought. Ferris wasn't that partial to her name, but didn't think our parents would let us trade. Anyway, she guessed she'd gotten used to it by now and didn't know if she could get used to being called something else. I liked the name of our town, too: Gilead. Mama said the name came from the bible, and meant a place where one could find solace.

I wished I could stay here by the pond and thought about hiding here in the woods until the family had left for the wedding. It would be worth getting a licking if I didn't have to wear those clothes. Everyone there would notice me in those clothes. "See there," they would think, smiling, "we knew Iris would come around, turn into a lady." It was like admitting I wasn't any stronger or more different than other girls when I had been trying to prove for years that I was. About the only good thing I could think of about the wedding was that Lucien was coming to it.

I was so busy worrying about the wedding that I almost stepped on the eggs. We'd been pushing through the old cattail stalks along the pond and then they seemed to explode in my face as a blue heron beat her great wings in alarm. She glided over the pond, and landed again to watch us. Three pale eggs lay at my feet. We'd startled her from her nest.

Mama was calling me. She had a clear voice that carried like a bell.

"Iris Anderson, I know you're hiding down there. You come this minute," and then she added, "Lucien's home."

"See ya tomorrow," Ferris said and headed home. I backed out of the cattails as quickly as I could and began to run.

I was glad I did, not because I was on time for the wedding, but for what happened when I got home.

I could tell Mama was angry with me, but Father had a twinkle in his eye. He looked uncomfortable in his suit and was already tugging at his tie. Mama ordered me to go get dressed.

"Before she does, I want to give Iris her present," Father said.

"Shouldn't we do that later?" Mama fretted. "I don't want us to be late."

"It'll just take a minute," Father said. "And maybe it'll make the wedding a little easier for her to sit through."

Father led us to the barn. I couldn't imagine why he'd

hidden my present out there, or what it could be. Like I'd said, I wasn't expecting much.

Father stopped by one of the box stalls.

"It's in here," he said. I peered over the top board of the stall and caught my breath.

Two Jersey calves, as small and delicate as fawns, lay curled in the hay.

"I saw Ned Stevens in town yesterday and he mentioned that one of his cows had had twins," Father said, grinning. "Happy Birthday, Iris."

Chapter Two

I sat through the wedding and thought of how miserable I felt. I wasn't trying to get over it; I was concentrating on it, storing up all the anger and humiliation I felt and picking at it like a scab, so I wouldn't forget this torture Mama had inflicted on me. I would hold this against her for a long time. But I blamed Aunt Lurdine, too. At least I had my calves to think about. I couldn't wait to get back and pet them.

With all the excitement, I hadn't told Lucien about the heron eggs. He'd given me a smile and a hug, while Mama gave me a dark look and hustled me off to my room to get dressed. I came out ten minutes later feeling as trussed up as a turkey. I was embarrassed for Lucien to see me, but he'd sensed how uncomfortable and angry I was and hadn't told me I looked beautiful or anything stupid like that.

In our family, it was just Father and Mama, Lucien and me, and there was seven years difference between him and me. Growing up with him had been tough. Lucien hadn't even known I existed, except to order me around, punch me, or lock me in the root cellar. Once he'd even pushed me through the kitchen window and Mama had spanked me for breaking it. And Lucien never called me by name; it was "Kid, go get the cows," or "Kid, get me a glass of milk," and even, "Go drown, kid." Then Lucien had gone to college and a wonderful thing had happened. When Lucien came home, I was suddenly important to him. He'd come home in the fall and walk to the pasture with me. The grasses and trees almost pulsed with color, and the raspy sawing of locusts filled our ears as we climbed. Bright monarch butterflies, moving like bobbers on water, fed on goldenrod and blue disks of aster that glowed in the golden light. The trees edging the pasture drooped with their loads of chokecherries, butternuts, and apples, and the heavy sweetness of bruised and decayed fruit rose from the grass as we walked near. I was sure spring was my favorite season until I was wrapped in fall's crisp days and starlit nights, and the kaleidoscope of color that made everything so bright, so alive, it seemed to glow from within. I was always caught in a flurry of emotions; an ache from too much beauty at one time and a feeling that the season was spinning past and I hadn't had time enough to enjoy it.

"I sure have missed this," I heard Lucien whisper. He was staring out over the valley, and he'd looked away but not before I caught the glint of tears in his eyes. I hadn't meant to stare, but it just about bowled me over, seeing that Lucien had some of the same feelings I did. He'd blinked quickly and picked up some crab apples that had fallen.

"Wanna help me make cider tomorrow?" he'd asked and out of the blue he'd started telling me about his classes, the books he was reading, which teachers he liked and which ones were jerks. And what was even more amazing was that he started asking me questions. Were there any boys I was interested in? NO. What sports did I like best, how many home runs had I scored? At first I was shy, not knowing if he was just teasing me again, but I started telling him more and more, and he listened to it all and didn't laugh once.

The wedding was long and boring and I dreaded the reception, but I did have to admit that Aletta was beautiful. She stood next to her new husband, flushed and eyes glittering with excitement, and she looked as sleek and dark as a barn swallow. Next to her, Aunt Lurdine reminded me of a blue jay, dressed real showy, but loud and annoying. She loved being the center of attention, too, just like a jay. Me, I looked like a heron, tall and gawky, with a too long nose, and knees and elbows that stuck out in all directions.

I figured I was the only one at the reception who was having a rotten time, until my cousin Draper came and sat next to me. He didn't look much happier than I felt, and when he sat, he tugged at his tie. Uncle Sturgis and Aunt Lurdine had four children: Walter and Margaret, both married, Aletta, and Draper, who'd been a real surprise, Father said. Father thought Draper was spoiled.

"I hate this," Draper said.

"I hate it more than you do. I'd do anything to wear what you're wearing."

"You've always hated dresses," Draper said. How could I tell him the dress was the most comfortable thing I had on?

"Your mom is trying to make me be a lady." I don't think I was able to keep the bitterness out of my voice.

Draper nodded sympathetically.

"You know Mom," he said.

I did, but I didn't say anything. I'd found out that kids

will say lots of things about their parents, but they don't want someone else running them down.

"Dear friends and honored guests," Aunt Lurdine hollered across the room, in a high singsong voice. Draper and I rolled our eyes at each other. "Please be seated for the luncheon." I didn't know anyone except Aunt Lurdine who used the word luncheon.

We sat at a table in the corner. I figured Aunt Lurdine was trying to hide us poorer relatives, but I was glad we were in the corner. On each table was a platter of little sandwiches shaped like hearts, and that was surrounded by crystal dishes filled with pickles and relishes. Aunt Lurdine was a compulsive canner and she had used Aletta's reception as a chance to show off her creations. There were dill beans and carrots, pickled beets, corn relish, beet relish, green tomato pickles, and ripe cucumber pickles.

Father leaned toward Mama.

"Is there any real food around here?" he whispered. "Everything here is pickled."

"Shh," Mama whispered back. "You can eat when we get home. At least have some of the cake."

"Is that pickled, too?" Father asked and Mama kicked him under the table.

He was right to be cautious. Aunt Lurdine wasn't a bad cook, but she had a bad habit of putting things together that should never go together. Like Jell-O and mayonnaise, squash and peanut butter, and the worst was her tuna pineapple salad. I don't know of anyone who ever took more than one bite of that salad. But, still, Aunt Lurdine thought she was a gourmet. I was sure that Aletta had prayed someone else would do the cooking for her wedding.

Aunt Lurdine swooped over.

"Everything went beautifully," Mama told her and Aunt Lurdine beamed.

"Yes, it did go swimmingly, didn't it?" she said, and looked at me. "Oh, Iris," she oozed. "Why, I hardly recognized you. Don't you look lovely?"

I wanted to choke her.

"But you know you really shouldn't wear green," she continued. "Pink would look so much better on you."

"I hate pink," I said through clenched teeth.

Aunt Lurdine acted like she hadn't heard me.

"Perhaps Aletta has some old dresses you could wear."

"No," I almost shouted, and everyone in the room stopped talking and turned to look at me. Aletta had a worried look and in a few moments she'd probably come over to see what was causing all the commotion. This was her day, and the last thing I wanted to be was the center of attention. I scrunched down into my chair, hoping the floor would open and swallow me in one quick gulp.

"She really doesn't like pink," my mother ventured apologetically. Oh, why couldn't she really stand up to Aunt Lurdine?

Aunt Lurdine pursed her lips.

"I declare, Edith, she's just a child. You shouldn't let her have her way so often. She's already too headstrong."

The words bubbled up in my throat to tell Aunt Lurdine I wasn't a child. I was thirteen years old now, but I felt Mama's hand tighten on my knee and took that as a warning to hold my tongue.

"Is it time to cut the cake?" someone asked, and Aunt Lurdine squealed and scurried off to hog the attention.

"Hope she cuts her throat," I muttered.

"Iris!" Mama scolded, "Lurdine means well."

"Lurdine," Father said, "means for everything to go just the way she wants it."

We sat through the cake-cutting, and the cake-eating. We sat through the photo-taking and bouquet-tossing, and we waited while Aletta changed clothes and the couple had driven away in a car, dragging the customary cans and old boots.

"Can we go home now?" I asked. I wanted to see my calves.

"Not yet," Mama said. "I'll be helping Lurdine clean up afterward."

"I was thinking of going home myself," Lucien said. "What if Iris comes with me, and I'll come back later to pick you up?"

"I guess that'd be all right," Mama said, and I silently thanked Lucien for rescuing me.

Father decided he'd had enough of weddings and receptions, too, and was only too glad to escape to the car with us. I wanted to talk with Lucien but knew he'd be close-mouthed and on edge with Father there.

There was tension, almost like static electricity, between Lucien and Father. They'd never sat me down to explain it to me, but I had a pretty good idea of what caused it. I'd heard Mama and Father arguing about it one night after they thought I'd gone to sleep.

Father had always planned that Lucien would take over the farm, but he hadn't planned on Lucien having ideas of his own. Lucien wanted to be a writer. In high school, he'd sent off one of his stories to *Field and Stream* and they had published it, calling it "realistic drama," or something like that. Even then, Lucien hadn't told Father. The first hint

Father had had of his plans was when Zeeb Gilman cornered him down at McCormick's Feed Store and told him, "That story your son wrote was the best fishing story I ever read." Father had come home, mad that nobody had told him about the story, but proud, too. It hadn't worried him, yet, because he still believed Lucien's writing was just a phase, and that Lucien would give it up soon and settle down to take over the farm.

Lucien never would have admitted it, but I think he was scared, not so much of challenging Father, but of challenging Father's plans for him. He must have known he was really going to hurt Father.

I was scared of Lucien then. He was so confused and angry and I was the easiest person for him to take out his anger on. He'd hit me anytime I walked by, so I was careful to keep my distance. Sometimes even that wasn't enough.

We were getting the cows one evening, and Lucien noticed that Molly was missing. He hollered over to me.

"Molly's gone. Must have had her calf. Go down into the swamp and find her."

The last thing I wanted to do right then was slog through the swamp in the dark, looking for a cow that didn't want to be found. So, without really thinking I told him, "Find her yourself." Next thing I knew a rock thudded into my back.

I yelped and jumped as the next one whizzed by my ear. Lucien began chucking rocks at my head, and I could tell by the look on his face he wasn't trying to miss. That scared me, knowing that he really meant to hurt me.

I ran. Lucien could have easily caught me, but he couldn't just leave the cows, so he let me go. I outran the range of his arm, and kept running until I reached the safety of the haymow.

The next day I heard Lucien talking to his friend, Telfer.

"Where you going to go?" Telfer asked.

"Don't know," Lucien said, "but anywhere's gotta be better than here. I can't live around my father anymore," and I had known he was going to run away. I waited until Telfer left, then followed Lucien to the toolshed. He was furious that I'd spied on him. He clenched a fist under my nose.

"If you tell Father, I'll squash you like a bug."

For once his threat seemed pale next to the bigger threat of our family destroyed.

"Lucien, you can hit me as much as you want if you just won't run away."

I think I'll always remember that look on Lucien's face. I heard his quick intake of air and he just stared at me for the longest time. Maybe that's when he really saw me for the first time ever. He never hit me again. And he hadn't run away. He and Father had lived an uneasy truce through the next year until he'd gone to college.

Lucien had become my friend, but I wondered if he and Father would ever be able to get along. Even now, as we rode home together from the reception, you could have spooned the tension into bowls, it was so thick. When they spoke to each other, it was like watching boxers sparring, the way they danced around, on their guard, careful not to expose anything vital.

It made me sad to see how the tension had driven them apart. As a child, Lucien had tagged along behind Father to help with farmwork, but they'd enjoyed other activities together: camping, fly-fishing, and baseball. Father had always loved baseball. He could rattle off batting averages for hundreds of players and listened to Red Sox games on the radio on Sunday afternoons. Even though the Red Sox hadn't won the World Series since 1918, Father would announce every spring that "this would be the year the Red Sox went all the way."

Father still played town ball in the summers. Lucien had played, too, for a couple of seasons, but last summer he'd chosen to work instead to earn his college tuition, and now he rooted for the Brooklyn Dodgers. It was another sore point between them.

"Sold any more stories?" Father asked. There was challenge in his voice.

Lucien gripped the steering wheel a little tighter and stared straight ahead.

"It takes time," he said.

Father snorted, "Waste of time, if you ask me."

"I didn't," Lucien said, icily, and we rode the rest of the way home in silence.

CHAPTER THREE

As soon as I'd changed out of the wedding clothes, I felt 100 percent better. I shoved the bra and nylon stockings way back under my bed. I hoped mice would find them and chew them to bits.

I ran to the barn and snuggled in the hay with my calves. I couldn't believe they were mine. I'd feed them, raise them, maybe even show them at the county fair. And once they started producing milk, in two years time, I'd start making some money.

When it was time to get the cows, I whistled for Gretel, our border collie, and headed up behind the pond.

"Hey, wait up," called Lucien. He ran across the yard and fell into step beside me. "Believe it or not, I've kinda missed getting the cows. Don't want to get out of practice."

We were skirting the pond, and I thought of the heron's nest. I told Lucien about the three eggs.

"I'd like to see them," he said, "but I don't want to scare her. If we're quiet around here this summer, we may be able to watch the chicks grow up."

We met the cows filing down the cowpath off Beech Hill. Cows are dumb, but they're creatures of habit and always know when it is time to be milked. Gretel circled around behind the stragglers, nipping a few heels and dancing out of the way when one of the cows kicked at her. They all stopped to drink at the brook and Lucien counted them off. We were a cow shy.

"Belle's missing. Must have had her calf."

I thought back to another time, looking for another calf when Lucien chucked that rock at my head. Things sure can change.

"I'll go back for her," Lucien said. "Hope I find her quick. I've got plans tonight."

"You going out?" I asked. I didn't know Lucien had a girl-friend.

Lucien nodded and my heart sank. I'd hoped he'd be home tonight and all the family would be together. Then he turned to me and smiled. "With you," he said. "After your birthday supper, how'd you like to sleep out up on the hill?"

I hurried through chores so fast that evening that Father looked at me strangely, and asked if my pants were on fire.

"No," I laughed. "Lucien and I are camping out tonight."

"Must be an epidemic," Father said. "Draper said he and a couple of his friends were fixing to sleep out. Wondered could they bed down up in the sugarwoods."

Funny, Draper hadn't said anything about that at the wedding. I started to feel miffed at not being invited, then realized that I was happier to be camping out with Lucien.

I fed both my calves with a bottle, bedded them down with some extra hay and petted them good night. I'd been thinking all day what I would name them, but hadn't found the perfect names for them yet. Maybe Lucien would help me decide on names tonight.

Lucien and I hurried through supper, too, and it was just turning dark when we'd gathered together what we needed and headed for the hill.

Most of the path was lost in shadows, but Lucien didn't turn on the flashlight and I was glad. I felt a part of the shadows and the soft, still air, and knew my feet would find the path by instinct. I think Lucien felt the same, for he moved quietly and paused often to listen to the night sounds: the trilling of tree frogs, and a barred owl calling *hoohoo-hoohoo, hoohoo-hoohooaw.*

We spread our sleeping bags on grass that had already been flattened by deer lying on it.

"We might see some come early morning," Lucien said. "They spend most nights up here, away from people. Might see some fawns too."

The sky to the west was flushed with color, dusky like the darker wild roses, and the spine of the Green Mountains was etched bold against it. Only the narrowest slice of moon hung in the west.

Just like in years past, when we'd been out haying past dark, hurrying to get the bales in before the next day's predicted rain, Lucien pointed out the stars and constellations to me, the old standbys of Cassiopeia, Cygnus the Swan, and the Northern Crown, and a few more that I didn't know: Hercules, Aquila the Eagle, and the Dolphin.

"And there's Bernice's Hair," Lucien said, pointing to a faint group of stars next to the brilliant star Arcturus. "It's the farthest constellation from the Milky Way."

We heard the *peent-peent* of woodcocks searching for mates and the wild jungle call of snipe. I could hardly believe it when Lucien told me that what we heard wasn't the snipe's call at all but was air passing through its tail feathers, but I knew Lucien knew about birds. There wasn't much that Lucien didn't know about, it seemed to me, and I loved it when he'd talk to me about the habits of birds and animals, or some history of our ancestors, or legends about the stars. When I said I wished we'd see northern lights tonight, Lucien told me the ancient Finns had believed the northern lights to be foxes with glistening fur running over the mountains. I loved that idea, and pictured them running through the sky as the night wrapped itself around us.

"With all the advances they're making in science these days, someday they'll send men to the moon."

I grinned into my sleeping bag. Sometimes Lucien had the strangest notions. Imagine, men on the moon. Still, what would it be like to fly through space, past the stars and planets?

Lucien brought me back to earth.

"If you could go anywhere in the world, where would you go?" he asked.

I thought hard. "I guess I don't want to go anywhere. I like it best right here on the farm."

"Ah, Iris, dream a little."

"Where do you want to go?" I asked.

"Anywhere. Everywhere. Alaska, New Zealand, Africa, China. One of my friends in college took the train across Canada and hiked for a month in the Rockies. I'd love to do that."

That did sound fun. Would Lucien and I ever do something like that together? Would he ever want to take along his sister?

I fell asleep and dreamed of running through singing

grass alongside foxes with fur that gleamed like silver in the starlight.

The first crack of thunder almost lifted me from the ground, and streamers of lightning, slicing the darkness, seemed ready to rip the sky to shreds. The violent beauty of the storm terrified me; I stared at the sky, half-expecting the heavens to open and we would hear the voice of God.

The air felt so charged I wouldn't have been surprised to see sparks fly off each blade of grass, and the hair on my neck stood up. Lucien didn't have to tell me we had to get off the hill. Up here we were begging to get struck down. I grabbed the sleeping bag and ran lickety-split down the trail. Every few seconds, lightning lit up the sky like daylight, but then plunged us back into darkness as it passed. I lost count of how many times I fell but I didn't stop to check for blood. I could count cuts and bruises tomorrow, if I didn't break a leg first, and if I didn't get fried to a crisp by a lightning bolt.

I was to the brook before I heard Lucien hot on my heels and knew he'd taken a few extra seconds to grab the canteen and flashlight. For the first time, I wondered if Draper and his friends had made it to shelter before the storm struck.

Mama met us at the door. "Thank goodness you're here," she said. "I tried to send your father out after you, but he said no sense him getting drenched when the two of you would just be hightailing it back here."

And drenched we were. We couldn't have been wetter if either of us had been thrown in the pond with our clothes on. I was bleeding in a few places too where I'd fallen and roots and branches had snagged me, but they weren't much and I was shaking all over more from relief to be home than from cold or hurts or anything.

Mama made kind of a party of it, heating up some milk for cocoa while we changed, and toweling off my hair next to the stove. She said the thunder was too loud for anybody to sleep anyway, and Lucien made us laugh telling how I'd abandoned him on the hill and galloped faster than Ichabod Crane's headless horseman on the way down.

The storm passed over about as quickly as it had come and by the time we fell into bed again, Lucien said you could even see a few stars to the west. Mama tucked me in, something she hadn't done for years and, where I might have felt too grown up for that any other night, tonight I liked it.

"Guess we've had enough excitement for one night," Mama said and kissed me.

I'm not sure I dreamed anything then. But I woke with a sour taste in my mouth from the cocoa, and wondered why the windows were glowing. And before I had shrugged off sleep, I heard Mama's scream.

"Hazen! The barn's on fire!"

CHAPTER FOUR

I guess we all knew from the first there was no saving it. By the time we'd all rushed outside, clothes hanging ragtag, the doors and windows were choked with flames, and sparks were spraying over us like rain. Worst of all, over the roar and crackle of the flames came the screams of the cows trapped inside.

I'll never forget the look on Father's face, a terrible look that burned with the intensity of the fire. Mama saw it, too, and clutched at his arm.

"You can't, Hazen. Let them go. They're not worth dying for." But she knew Father couldn't let them go without trying. He yanked his arm free, Mama screaming his name, and ran for the barn. He ran through the flaring doorway and it seemed he'd been swallowed by a furnace.

Mama ran after him. I grabbed her shirttail and dug my heels into the dirt. She tried to shake me off, yelling at me to let go, and when I didn't, she twisted and started hitting at my arms. I couldn't protect myself without letting go, so I dove in toward her, wrapping my arms around her waist, and buried my face in her shirt. My nose was running, I was crying, begging her to stay with me, and I was more scared than I'd ever been in my life. We were both crazy from fear, not knowing what we were doing or saying. I guess my crying finally got through. Mama kind of shook herself, then grabbed me and held me to her and I knew she wasn't crazy anymore.

We heard yelling and saw some cows tumble out of the side door. A dark figure followed them, yelling and beating at them when they tried to turn back. I'd heard that cows and horses will run right back into a burning barn, and I'd always found it hard to believe, but now I could see it for myself. The cows were jumping around and bellowing and the figure was running after them and it was Lucien. I hadn't had time to think where Lucien had been, and I'm ashamed to say I hadn't even worried about him, but I was glad he was safe.

Lucien got the cows headed off at a run toward the brook, then broke away from them, running past us toward the house. I was too stunned to think about what he might be doing. When he came back out, he had Father's gun.

Mama and I stood together, our eyes riveted on the doorway where Father had disappeared. We were too scared to think, and even if we could have thought, we didn't want to. We knew Father had been in there too long. Images of him flashed through my head, like a movie, of him trapped in the flames, choking and blinded by smoke, unable to find the door and finally falling to the floor as he cried out our names. There was no way he could live in that heat, and then he appeared in the doorway, he and our horse, Bennington, silhouetted against that savage orange glow, black images as if already charred. Father's shirt was over Bennington's head, but even so, Bennington was almost lifting Father off the ground as he reared and screamed. Father's hair was singed, his eyebrows burned off, and he was gulping great drafts of air. But he was alive.

When Father was in the yard, Lucien sighted down the barrel and began firing into the windows. I couldn't figure out what he was doing and then it dawned on me he was trying to kill the cows before the fire got to them. I hid my face against Mama.

At the first crack of the gun, Father's head reared back. His eyes had a wild, hunted look. Mama ran to him.

"Thank God," Mama said. "Hazen, are you all right?"

I don't think Father even heard her. He was coughing hard, and when he did speak, his voice was cracked and harsh from the smoke he'd breathed.

"I got four out. And three of the calves. But I couldn't save the rest of them," and his eyes flooded with tears. For the first time ever, I saw my father cry.

Mama meant to offer comfort.

"Lucien got out quite a few," she said.

Lucien lifted the rope from Father's hand to lead Bennington away. It was the first any of us had noticed that he'd stopped shooting. He shook his head.

"I could only reach the ones on the end," he said. "I only got out eight." That meant Ginger was out. She was on the end. But only eight. I thought of the others, Beth, Ellen, and gentle Molly, all of them gone. I'd seen them all just a few hours ago, alive and warm and comforting as home-made bread. I'd even scratched Molly's neck on my way to feed the calves.

"My calves!" I cried, searching Lucien's face. "Did you get out my calves?"

Lucien lifted his eyes to me, pity etched on his face, and shook his head. Pain bit into me like a knife. My sweet calves. I hadn't even named them yet.

We watched as the barn began to collapse, like an old dog that sinks painfully to its haunches. The white letters on the barn that spelled Scottish Hills Farm were curled and brown, and then the flames ate them, too. By the time the roof had fallen in, we heard the fire engine coming from Gilead, climbing the long hill to our farm. No one counted on the fire department. Father called them Gilead's cellar-savers, but I didn't know why they were bothering to come. The barn didn't have a cellar, so there was nothing to save this time.

As it turned out, cars and people came and went for the rest of the night. I wished they'd never come. There wasn't anything to save, and we couldn't even act natural and grieve for our cows and beautiful barn with all those people around.

All our neighbors were there, the men clustered around Father, staring at the ruins, stiff and silent as stones. The women were more vocal, swarming around Mama like bees. Though I'd rather have been left alone, I couldn't really hold any hard feelings against any of them; they were just being good neighbors. It was something that was just understood in Gilead; if someone had a fire, or an accident, or a death in the family, you went to them and stayed, whether you could help or not.

The people I wanted to scream at were the ones who'd driven from towns as far away as Sutton, Irasburg, and Eden, just to see the ruins. They'd pull into the yard, staring and pointing at the smoldering pile that had been our barn, then leave, waving at us as if we were just one more stop on a tour. I could just see them wishing they'd been here to see the fire. I wanted to grab the post maul and whang them all over the head. Made me mad, them using our misfortune for their own entertainment.

Just as the sky started to lighten, folks began to leave, heading back to their own barns for morning chores. Father quietly thanked them all for coming, his voice still harsh from breathing in smoke. I couldn't bear to look at him, his face covered with soot, and his eyes mournful as a hound's.

When the last car left, Mama hustled us into the house. She wanted me to lie down for some rest, but I couldn't bear to go to my room all alone, so she sat on the couch, and I lay with my head on her lap. I didn't figure I'd ever fall asleep, I was so tore up inside, but I was also exhausted and without knowing it, I fell into a sleep filled with cows and horses and my calves screaming and bursting into flames until I woke up screaming, too. The tears came then, and I cried myself back to sleep while Mama smoothed my forehead with her cool hand.

CHAPTER FIVE

Maybe if I didn't open my eyes, or look out the window, it wouldn't have happened. The barn would still be standing, red as an apple, the cows bellowing to get milked, Sasparilla, the barn cat, curling around Father's legs, begging for a taste of warm milk. Then the wind brought me the smell of smoldering hay and burnt flesh.

Breakfast was a miserable affair. None of us had gotten much sleep and no one was hungry. Mama didn't even make us go to church. I could tell she'd been crying, and Lucien wasn't telling his stories that always made us laugh.

All day, we didn't know what to do with ourselves. Our natural rhythms and habits had been disrupted. Out in the yard, Lucien and Father hand-milked the cows we had left, then let them out to pasture. Father got out the bulldozer and began burying the charred carcasses and remains of the barn. I didn't think I'd want to watch, but I was drawn to the yard by some grim fascination. I didn't get too close. The stench from the cows made me gag, and I wondered how Father could work in that mess. It frightened me to look at Father. He looked like a man who'd lost everything.

Ferris came over, but I didn't feel much like talking.

"Let's just go for a walk," she said. "We don't have to talk." We headed off across the yard toward the orchard, and that's when I found it.

I was kicking through the mud by the Duchess apple tree when something shiny caught my eye. I reached down to pick it up and my breath caught in my throat. It was Draper's jackknife.

"Who's is that?" Ferris asked.

"Mine," I lied. I hadn't meant to. I just needed time to think about this, and what it meant. "I lost it awhile ago."

She looked at me curiously, and I knew she was probably wondering why she'd never seen the knife if it had been mine, but she didn't ask any more questions. I slid the jackknife into my pocket, and we went for our walk.

After supper, I cornered Lucien in the pantry.

"What do you think caused the fire?" I asked him.

He shrugged.

"Don't know," he said. "A good guess would be lightning hit the barn, though the firemen said they couldn't tell. At least we know it wasn't combustion of the hay, since last year's hay's mostly gone. Might have been wiring. Who knows?"

That's what I wondered.

"Could someone have set it?"

Lucien looked at me more carefully.

"You have some special reason for asking?"

"No," I blurted out, a little too quickly. "I was just wondering."

"I hadn't really considered that," Lucien said slowly. "I can't imagine someone setting it. Who would want to do that to us?"

"Oh, nobody," I said. I was sorry now I'd brought it up. "I guess it must have been an accident, after all."

Lucien looked like he was about to ask me something else, so I hurried outdoors before he could. I needed time to sort through my thoughts before I began accusing people.

Somehow, we managed to get through the day, but I dreaded the night. I didn't want to close my eyes. I was afraid the house would catch fire while I slept, trapping us inside, and imagined the flames creeping closer, lapping at us. Mama sat with me again, stroking my head and humming till I fell asleep. And when I woke up later in the night, crying, she lay beside me and held me.

Mama didn't call me in the morning and by the time I woke up, I'd missed the bus. Mama didn't even offer to drive me to school and I was grateful she didn't make me go; I still wasn't ready to face all the attention at school that I knew the fire would generate.

Father wasn't at the breakfast table.

"He's up on the ridge, cutting wood," Mama explained.

"Cutting wood?" Lucien asked. "You mean firewood?"

"No," Mama said. "He's cutting wood for a new barn."

Lucien and I looked at each other, then he strode outside quickly. I followed him at a trot. He milked the cows as quickly as he could, though hand-milking is a pretty slow process. I tried to help, milking Ginger and Belle in the time it took him to milk all the others, and he stripped out the last milk from the two I'd done. Then Lucien went to the toolshed for the heavy double-bladed ax that was hard for me to even lift.

"Take them out to pasture, will you?" he said to me, nodding toward the cows, and headed off to join Father.

Father and Lucien cut wood all day, Father sawing

down the trees and Lucien limbing them. Father used Bennington to skid out the logs. Bennington had a few spots on his back where embers had burned away the hair, and he was still jumpy, but he was a good steady horse and a hard worker.

With Father and Lucien busy in the woods, I had some free time, and I went back to check on the heron nest. I tried not to get too close and scare the mother, but she saw me, or heard me, and came hissing at me, her big wings flapping, and jabbing her long, powerful beak. I got out of there fast but not before I'd seen the three baby birds. I knew they'd grow into beautiful herons, but right now, they were the ugliest little birds I'd ever seen. So ugly they were cute.

Our barn fire was the talk of the school on Tuesday. Some kids, unsure of what to say, avoided me altogether, but those less shy kept rushing up, asking me was it true my brother had died in the fire, and hadn't my father escaped by jumping on a horse and riding from the burning barn with his shirt in flames and the firemen had had to hose him down? Just goes to show you how rumors get started.

Throughout the day, I kept Draper's jackknife in my pocket. I think I hoped by carrying it, it would whisper up its secret to me, a secret I wasn't sure I wanted to know.

Excitement began to wane after a couple of days, and just when most of the talk died down, we were surprised one morning to find a new girl in our class.

We all stared at her as if she'd just flown in from Mars. We'd never had a new kid in school. All the kids in my class were the same kids I'd been with since first grade, children of farmers whose families had lived in Gilead for near two hundred years.

The teachers never changed either. There was old Mrs. Randolph who was deaf in one ear and looked like she'd taught school since the Revolutionary War. She taught English and history, and Mr. Collier taught science and arithmetic. Mr. Collier claimed to be muscle-bound, but anyone could see he was just fat. His favorite topic in science was food. He also claimed he was teaching us about nutrition, but we figured it was because he liked to eat. He told us about vitamins and minerals we needed, like iron.

"All growing girls need iron," Mr. Collier said.

"Not Iris," said Johnson Gates, who I'd walloped during recess when he tried to take my outfielder's glove away. It had been Grandpa's glove, and I wasn't about to let Johnson get his slimy hands on it.

Anyway, the new girl's name was Alice Mitchell. Her dress was thin and faded, her shoes had holes, and her face carried a pinched, hungry look.

I should have said hello, asked where she was from, invited her to eat lunch with Ferris and me out under the lilac bush, but I didn't. I didn't want anything to do with her. The fire had left me feeling mean, and sorry for myself. I guess I wanted to take those feelings out on somebody and who better than a new kid?

"I bet she's got lice," I whispered to Ferris, and Ferris giggled. I didn't care if Alice heard me or not.

Mrs. Randolph put her in the empty seat right in front of me. I didn't want her there and decided to let her know it. Several times during the day I kicked her seat, and pulled her hair and after lunch, Ferris and I put a garter snake in her desk. Then we sat back to watch what would happen.

Alice came in from recess with the other kids and sat

down. Mrs. Randolph asked everyone to get out their history books. Ferris and I held our breaths as Alice opened her desk. Alice jumped a little, and shut her desk quickly, but she didn't scream or anything. I looked at Ferris and shrugged. We'd hoped for a livelier reaction but I had to give Alice credit. She wasn't a sissy.

Somehow, Mama found out about Alice's arrival.

"I hear there's a new girl in your class," she said at supper.

I looked guiltily at Mama. Had she heard about some of the mean things I'd done to Alice?

"I wonder where they're living," Mama mused. "I haven't heard of any new family in town. Do you know where they live?"

I shook my head.

"Well, if you find out, let me know," Mama said. "I want to invite them over for supper some night."

I made up my mind right then and there that I wouldn't tell Mama even if I did find out where Alice lived. I didn't want her and her whole dirty family coming to our house.

By Saturday, I realized I hadn't seen Draper all week which was strange. He usually came over every couple of days to play. Before the fire, he and I would build hay forts in the barn, or build dams along the brook, or look for the cave on the other side of Beech Hill that Grandpa had told us had been used by smugglers to hide goods during the War of 1812, and later, as a hiding place for runaway slaves on the Underground Railroad. Grandpa had never gotten around to showing us where it was. Someday, I'd hunt it up, but not with Draper. If what I suspected was true, I wouldn't be playing with Draper anymore.

I wished I had someone to share my suspicions with and I thought about telling Ferris—I told her all my secrets—

but something kept me quiet about this. Maybe it was because Draper was family. Or maybe it was because I didn't want to believe myself that Draper could have done such a thing.

There I was, walking along the brook, thinking about the knife and what I was going to do about it, and along came Draper, just the person I'd been thinking of. He was carrying a fishing pole.

When he saw me, he turned as if to go off in the other direction, but he must have figured I'd already seen him, and it'd look suspicious if he just took off. He started whistling, a little too loudly, and walked up beside me. He was all smiles, but something in my face must have alerted him because he stopped smiling when I pulled his knife out of my pocket.

"Where'd you find it," he asked carefully.

"In the ashes," I said. I was watching his face and the fear in his eyes told me more than I wanted to know.

"Why'd you do it, Draper?" I asked, so quietly I wasn't sure he'd heard me. I surprised myself with the load of sorrow in my voice.

"It wasn't me, Iris," he said, scuffing his toes in the dirt. "I didn't do it."

"I found your knife there," I said. "You were there."

He opened his mouth, and I think he meant to lie to me, again, to say he'd lost the knife a long time ago. But he was a kid, after all, and he was scared.

"It was Jeff and Harley," he said. He still wouldn't look at me. "They had some cigarettes, and thought it'd be cool to smoke up in the barn, what with the rain washing out our camping trip and all. I knew it was stupid, and I wanted to tell them no, but they would've called me a chicken."

"Better to be called a chicken than what's gonna happen to you when your dad and mom find out."

"You can't tell anyone, Iris," Draper said wildly. His words tumbled out like water over a spill dam. "You can't. You know my mother. She'd kill me!"

"It isn't something like skipping school," I yelled. I was so mad red spots swam in front of my eyes. I couldn't believe my own cousin had caused all this trouble. "You burned our barn down, and those cows burned alive. Father was almost trapped in there, trying to get Bennington out. What if he'd died, too?"

"I know," Draper said, snuffling now and wiping his nose on his sleeve. "I'd do anything for it not to have happened, to bring your barn back. But you can't tell my mom. You wouldn't tattle, would you?"

He had me there. I hated tattletales. But I'd never had to keep such a big secret, or such a terrible one. It didn't seem fair.

"No, I ain't a tattletale," I said bitterly. "Or a coward and that's what you, and Jeff and Harley are. If I get asked who set the fire, I'll tell, 'cause I'm no liar either. But I wish you'd tell on your own."

"I will," Draper said eagerly, relieved now to know I wasn't about to squeal on him. "Someday, I will," but I couldn't say I believed him.

CHAPTER SIX

I went up on the ridge, one day, to see where Lucien and Father'd been cutting. While they loaded up the wagon, using cant hooks to roll the heavy spruce and fir logs onto the wagon bed, I wandered through the woods. A knot of hurt and hatred burned like a coal in my stomach, hatred for Draper and what he'd done. I didn't see how I'd ever keep his secret. I didn't want to keep it. I wanted Draper to be punished, but there wasn't any punishment bad enough for him as far as I was concerned.

The leaves were out full now, and the woods were shadowy and cool. I was just getting so I could tell a few birds by their songs, what with Lucien's help, and I recognized a veery and an ovenbird, and two other calls I knew to be warblers but I couldn't tell which ones. Someday, I'd be able to pick them all out of the air by their voices, just like Lucien did. My spirits lifted. Even with the barn gone, it was hard to feel sad on a day like this.

Father was talking with Lucien when I got back.

"If I'd had my druthers, I'd have cut these trees in February. Now's the worst time of year to be cutting timber, what with the sap in the wood, but I didn't know then that

I'd be needing a barn now. Leastways, we got it at the right time of the moon."

I knew Father and the other farmers around Gilead still farmed according to the moon. I figured some of Lucien's teachers at the college would have laughed at Father, but Father wasn't backward and I believed most of what he told me. I knew the best time for planting was two days before full moon, except for root crops like potatoes, carrots, turnips, and beets which should be planted during a waning moon. But I didn't know about cutting timber.

"Best to fell your trees just before a new moon," Father explained. "If you cut wood while the moon is waxing, it'll rot right quick on you." He looked sideways at Lucien.

"I 'spect they teach you different than that at college."

Lucien shrugged.

"What if they do?" he said. "Nothing I say would change your mind."

Father scratched Bennington's neck and looked at the load of logs.

"With what we've taken down to the mill already, this should be plenty, but I'll cut down a couple more just to be safe. Take this load to Piette's, then stop by the hardware and get me some extra blades for the cutter bar. We'll be mowing next week."

I rode with Lucien to the sawmill, and we picked up the cutter blades on the way home. Since Father wasn't back, we did chores together, Lucien milking while I fed. The cows had gotten pretty used to being milked outside and weren't in such a yank to kick. Without Father there, the chores took us twice as long, and dusk had just started to settle by the time we'd put the cows back out to pasture and went in to supper.

Mama was at the stove, stirring something.

"Is your father with you?" she asked.

"No," said Lucien. "He isn't back yet?"

Mama looked up then, concern in her eyes. She shook her head.

"Mm," said Lucien, "that's funny. He said he was only going to cut a couple more trees." But, then, seeing Mama's face, he added, "Oh, you know Father. On the way back, he probably found something else that needed doing."

We sat down to eat. Mama kept throwing worried looks at the clock and she just picked at her food. It didn't seem strange to me that Father was late. Father was late lots of times.

Lucien finished his shepherd's pie and stood up quickly.

"I'll go look for him," he said.

I scrambled to my feet, jostling the table and my glass of milk. "Me, too."

"You'll do no such thing," Mama said. "You'll finish the rest of your supper and go to bed."

"She could help me, Mama," Lucien said, and I wanted to hug him.

"Well, I don't know," Mama said. "I guess it's all right."

Lucien took a flashlight and I followed him across the brook, through the hardwoods to the ridge where the spruce and fir grew tall and straight, like the virgin timber the first settlers cut and sold for ship's masts, Lucien had told me. But, tonight, Lucien wasn't talking much, and I had to hustle to keep up with him.

"Like you said," I told him, "he probably just found another job to do."

"I don't know," he said, without slowing. "I have this funny feeling something's wrong."

I was surprised at his worry.

"He came out of the fire all right," I said. "Nothing can happen to him now."

Lucien stopped and spun around. "You think that's a guarantee that he'll live forever? Just because he was lucky there doesn't mean he couldn't be lying up here dead right now. Life doesn't work that way, Iris."

That scared me and shut me up, too.

We cut up along the ridge where I'd walked in the shadowy woods just hours before. The going was steep here, and we had to skirt around stumps and rocks. The air was rich with smells of cut wood and old leaves.

Lucien played his flashlight along the stumps till it shone on one tree tilted at an angle and we saw Father.

The tree Father had been cutting had kicked backward off its stump and pinned Father up against another tree. It mostly had him by the leg and that leg was chewed up like hamburger from what I could see. His face was ghostly white in the light, and I almost screamed when the light reflected in his eyes, eyes that burned like two red coals in the darkness.

"Dear God," Lucien breathed. We both stood as if rooted.

Father's voice came to us, twisted and terrible, not like Father's voice at all.

"I figured you'd find me," he whispered.

Lucien knelt beside him.

"I got myself in a bit of a fix," Father said. He tried to smile, but the pain twisted it into a snarl.

The bar of the chain saw was buried in the stump. After being pinned Father had tried sawing through the tree, but the tree had shifted and pinched the bar. Lucien knew he had to get the saw out to free Father, and he yanked and pulled with all his might, but the saw held fast.

"Hurry! Oh, please, Lucien, hurry!" I pleaded. I expected Father to die any minute. I didn't see how anyone could keep living with a leg in that shape. I didn't know how much blood there was in the human body, but most of Father's looked to be spilled out on last year's leaves. And I knew, as Lucien did, that we didn't have time to go back to the farm for a saw or a tractor or anything. By the time we got back, Father would be dead.

Lucien left off pulling on the saw and stood, breathing hard, his arms at his side.

"Oh, Lucien, what are we going to do? Please, please, get him out." Please, God, I prayed, don't let Father die.

Lucien clenched his fists once, then backed right up against the fallen tree. He squatted and placed his shoulder blades against the bark.

I knew Lucien was strong. On a bet from Telfer, I'd seen him carry 100-pound bags of grain in his teeth. Mama said he was built like her brother Harry who was the only man she knew who could lift a drum of syrup. Full syrup drums weighed almost three hundred pounds. But I knew even Lucien was not strong enough to lift that tree.

"You can't lift it," I cried. I was angry. I wanted Lucien to figure out what to do.

"I'm not going to lift it. I'm gonna just try to move it enough for you to pull Father out. Grab him under the arms and the minute I say so, you pull him clear."

I hesitated. Father seemed too horrible to touch.

"Damn it, Iris, move," Lucien barked, and I reached my arms around Father's chest. Father's head lolled against my neck and I shuddered as I saw, in the dim glow of the flashlight, that he'd bitten through his lower lip.

Lucien heaved and strained. The muscles in his shoulders and arms knotted and bulged until he looked like a workhorse. But nothing moved.

Lucien stood to rest. He looked at Father and his eyes burned with such concentration and determination that I knew Lucien would move the tree or die trying.

He squatted and put his back to the tree again. He dug his heels into the earth. He breathed deep, gathered his strength and heaved against the tree. I expected the muscles in his arms to pop, to come hissing through the skin like pieces of cut wire.

For a few more seconds nothing happened, and then the tree moved. Just a little, but it moved. Lucien dug his feet in deeper and began to straighten his powerful legs. The tree half-swung, half-rolled a few inches to the side and I felt Father sag in my arms.

"Now, Iris," Lucien hissed through his teeth.

I pulled so hard I almost fell backward, with Father on top of me, but I somehow managed to keep moving my feet and dragged Father away from the tree to a level spot some fifteen feet away. My adrenaline was pumping so hard I felt I could lug him for miles. Lucien eased off the tree and it swung back, thudding against the tree where Father had been pinned.

Lucien pulled on Father's boot. I had a horrible image of Father's leg coming off with the boot. Lucien must have had a similar thought, too, because he pulled out his jackknife and cut the boot off. Blood poured out onto the ground. I guess that's when Father passed out. I thought he was dead and started crying, but Lucien told me to shut up, he was just passed out.

"I need you to help me, not fall apart," he said. I didn't

say anymore except, "He gonna die, Lucien?" but Lucien wouldn't answer me.

We hadn't brought anything for first aid. Lucien ripped off his shirt and used it to wrap around Father's leg as a bandage. That was a little better, because it covered up the sight of that gruesome leg, or what was left of it, though looking at Father's face wasn't much comfort. Lucien placed branches beside Father's leg, one on each side, and used strips of his shirt to splint them to the leg.

I looked up into Lucien's face.

"Should I go get the tractor?" I asked him.

Lucien shook his head. "There isn't time," he said. "I'm going to carry him. Walk ahead of me with the light." He leaned over Father and grabbing Father's arm, he swung him over his shoulder, draping him like a U around his neck.

I walked ahead, playing the flashlight over the stumps, rocks, and fallen logs so Lucien wouldn't stumble and fall. I think Father was unconscious most of the way down which was a blessing. As careful as Lucien was being, it couldn't have been any too comfortable jouncing around on his shoulders.

As soon as we came off the hill into the pasture and more level ground, Lucien spoke again.

"Run ahead and have Mama get the car started. Then run down to Ora White's and have him call the hospital to tell them we're bringing Father in." I took off like a deer.

Mama was watching at the door for us and the minute she saw the flashlight, she ran toward me. I was shaking like a leaf and breathing hard, and I probably didn't make much sense, but Mama didn't waste time asking me questions about all that had happened.

Even though I thought she let Aunt Lurdine walk all over

her, Mama was strong and she didn't fall apart in a crisis. She ran to pull the car around front while I took off for Ora White's.

We didn't have a phone so I was used to carrying messages down to the Whites' for them to make a call for Mama or Father. Usually it was to the feed store to see if they had a part for some broken machinery. I wished that was all it was tonight.

I must have looked a sight, bursting in on the Whites without even knocking, covered with mud, blood, and bits of dead leaves. Mr. and Mrs. White both rose from their chairs at the sight of me.

"Mercy!" Mrs. White said. "What's wrong?" but Mr. White was already reaching for the phone.

Once the call was made, I didn't know what to do with myself. For the last hour or so, everything had been done in such haste, and now that there was nothing for me to do, my knees shook so hard I had to sit down.

Mrs. White fussed over me, bringing me a warm washcloth for my face and a glass of iced tea.

"You can stay right here with us, dear, until we hear from your mother," she said. I couldn't bear the thought of sitting in their living room all night, wondering what was happening at the hospital. I wanted to be with Lucien and Mama.

But Mr. White shook his head.

"No, Irene," he said to his wife. "If Iris was a little girl I'd agree with you. But right now, I think she needs to be with her family." I could have kissed him. He started up his dark green Chevy and drove me the twenty-five miles to the hospital in Hardwick.

Chapter Seven

I was old enough to be allowed into the hospital (kids under twelve weren't admitted) but Father was so badly hurt that they weren't letting any of us in to see him. I heard phrases like "arterial insufficiency" and "multiple compound fractures." This sounds awful, but I didn't really want to see Father. He was hurt bad, and I was afraid of what he might look like. I'd seen him out in the woods, his gray face twisted in pain, the flash of white bone poking through the bloody meat of his leg, and it had been enough. After that terrifying night in the woods, I was glad to have someone else taking care of him, doctors and nurses who knew how to take care of Father more than Lucien and I did.

Mama had called Aunt Lurdine to tell her about Father, and she and Uncle Sturgis and Draper had hustled right on over to the hospital. I was so worried about Father that I didn't even mind it when Aunt Lurdine showed up. She hugged Mama, and I could tell Mama was glad to have her there. But Draper wouldn't look at me.

We were all sitting in the waiting room, trying to think of

anything besides the possibility of Father dying and none of us succeeding.

Mama's voice startled us.

"Lurdine, you remember what Papa looked like?"

Aunt Lurdine looked at Mama like she'd gone crazy.

"Course I remember," she said. "How could I forget my own father?"

I'd gotten real still and was listening carefully. I knew what Mama meant. It was something I'd worried about, too, and felt guilty about.

"No, I mean really remember," Mama said. "It's something you think you can't ever forget, and it's scary when you realize you can. Because now his face is kind of blurry in my mind, and I can't remember exactly if his nose was long, or if his sideburns came down past his ears or just to the tips or . . ."

" . . . or if his eyes had green or brown flecks in them," I added.

Mama looked at me, and something passed between us then, an understanding of something deeper shared than what she had with her sister.

"I declare, I don't know what you're talking about," said Aunt Lurdine, and for once, I was glad she didn't. Mama squeezed my hand, and I squeezed back, glad to be beside her instead of back at the Whites' house.

Lucien wouldn't sit still. He paced around the room like a caged animal, watching the operating room door, then staring out the window.

"Boy makes me nervous," Uncle Sturgis muttered, but Lucien didn't hear.

"If only I'd been there," he kept saying, and he wouldn't

listen when I tried to tell him it wasn't his fault. I guess I wasn't understanding too well myself. Why had Father been saved from the fire, just to face death again a few weeks later? Was God playing a cruel joke on him? On me?

" . . . those boys came home looking like drowned rats," Aunt Lurdine was saying, and I realized she'd been telling Mama about Draper's camping trip. "They wouldn't admit it, but I think the lightning really scared them. They looked frightened. And then your barn burned. What a night! And now this. I declare, bad things do come in bunches."

I knew why Draper had looked scared that night. I glared at him and he squirmed. And when he went to the bathroom a few minutes later, I followed him. Draper's eyes widened in alarm when he saw me.

"Iris, you can't come in . . ." he started to say, but I grabbed the front of his shirt and shoved him against the wall.

"You just shut up," I said. I wanted to smash his face with my fist. "This is all your fault. Father never would have gotten hurt if you hadn't burned the barn down so he had to go cut that lumber. I hate you. You're the one that should be in the hospital, you're the one that should have been crushed under that tree after what you did. And you know what? I would have left you there, too." My voice had gotten higher and shriller as I yelled at him, and my arms shook. I'd never been so mad.

Draper started crying, big, gulping sobs that shook his body.

"Go ahead and cry, you sniveling brat. Maybe I won't squeal on you, but I'll tell you one thing. You're going to pay for this. If it's the last thing I do, I'm going to make you pay." I smacked him hard against the side of his head and left him still crying.

When I got back to the waiting room, I hoped no one would notice how upset I was. I was in no mood to lie for Draper.

"Where's Draper?" Aunt Lurdine asked.

"He went to the bathroom," I told her. At least that wasn't a lie.

Draper came back in a few minutes, looking terrible. His eyes were swollen from crying and I noticed one of his ears was red from where I'd smacked him. He still didn't look at me.

Aunt Lurdine gave a cry and crushed him in a hug.

"Goodness!" she said. "All this trouble's got you all worked up. My poor sweetheart! Sturgis, you take this boy home right now and put him to bed. He's too young for this sort of thing."

Uncle Sturgis studied Draper a moment, then gave me a long, appraising look. I felt my face grow hot and looked at the floor.

We were at the hospital all night. It was the longest night of my life. The doctors were operating on Father, trying to save his leg and his life, and all we could do was wait. I know Mama and Aunt Lurdine were praying up a storm, and I tried to, but my heart wasn't in it. I was too mad at Draper, and I was mad at God.

It was morning before one of the doctors came to see us. He pushed through the door, and we all turned toward him. I was afraid of what he had to say.

"He's in recovery right now," the doctor said to Mama. He looked tired, too. "He'll be asleep for another hour or so.

He's in serious, but stable, condition." Mama sagged against Aunt Lurdine, her face flooded with relief.

"Did you save the leg?" Lucien asked as if he had read my mind.

"For now," the doctor said, "but I don't want to build up your hopes. There was massive tissue damage, and we're not sure how successful we've been in reestablishing circulation throughout the limb. And there's still the huge risk of infection. It will be some time before we can be sure."

"Can I see him?" Mama asked.

"You'll need to wait until he's moved to a room. I suggest you all go home and get some sleep and come back to see him later." The doctor didn't know we lived twenty-five miles away, a long trip by way of rough dirt roads. And none of us wanted to leave without seeing for ourselves that Father was really alive. But Lucien surprised me by saying, "Mama, I'll go back and do the milking, then get back as soon as I can." I hadn't once thought of the chores to be done, that life was going on outside and all around us.

Mama hesitated, then nodded. I think she hated having Lucien leave.

"Can I bring you anything from home?" he asked her, and Mama listed off some things, from a toothbrush to a change of clothes. I realized then that Mama might be at the hospital a long time, until Father was out of danger.

"Iris, why don't you go with him?" Mama said tiredly. "I don't know how much longer it will be before we can see Father, and they'll probably only let me in to see him at first. You could help Lucien with the chores."

I wanted to stay with Mama, to hear for myself that Father was going to be all right, but Mama looked so tired I didn't argue.

Lucien and I had a quiet trip home. Lucien said once, "He'll be all right," mostly for my benefit, but I could tell he wasn't too sure himself, and I was glad he didn't try to cheer me up.

Lucien and I did the chores, then wandered about, trying to fill up time so we wouldn't think about Father, but it didn't work. I couldn't get the images from last night out of my head.

Mr. White drove over in the afternoon. Mama had called his place with a message for us. Father had woken up and spoken to her, but there wasn't any change in his condition and Mama felt there was no need for us to go back to the hospital today. She was going to stay there overnight and we could pick her up tomorrow.

Left alone, with only my thoughts, the afternoon yawned ahead of me like a chasm. I tried to read but couldn't focus on the words, walked out to the brook and around the fields, and finally it was time for evening chores. I was yawning so hard I thought my jaw would break. With everything that had happened, I'd forgotten Lucien and I hadn't had any sleep the night before. It was the first time I'd ever stayed up all night.

We each had a bowl of crackers and milk for supper, then I climbed the stairs to my dark bedroom. When the rural electrification program had come through the valley, Grandpa had only had the downstairs of the house wired. And Mama didn't dare let candles into the upstairs, so I was used to dressing in the dark. The upstairs wasn't heated, either. In winter, a glass of water left upstairs would freeze overnight. So in winter, I dressed under the covers.

Up until I was eight or so, Mama read to me every night, just as she had with Lucien, but because there was no light, she sat at the bottom of the stairs and read, her voice rising up the stairwell in the darkness, carrying with it all the images of cowboys and knights until it lulled me to sleep. Mama didn't believe in children's books; any book worth reading could be read to us, and characters like Natty Bumppo, Captain Ahab, and David Copperfield were as real and solid to me as granite.

I missed her voice tonight. The house seemed to echo with loneliness. I knew Father needed Mama at the hospital, but deep down inside I wanted her home. I was old enough to take care of myself, but tonight what I really wanted was to cuddle up next to her on the couch and have her read to me.

I slipped back downstairs and opened the door. Gretel lifted her head from her rug on the porch.

"Come on, girl," I whispered. Gretel looked at me without moving. She wasn't used to coming in. Mama didn't allow animals in the house, but Mama wasn't here tonight.

"It's all right, girl. You can come in." That was all the reassurance Gretel needed. She scooted in and followed me upstairs. With a little more coaxing, I got her onto the bed and with her warm body curled up next to mine, I managed to fall asleep.

CHAPTER EIGHT

Father stayed in intensive care for the next two weeks, while the doctors worked to save his leg, and Mama stayed with him, occasionally coming home for fresh clothes and a nap. She looked like she'd aged ten years, and with her gone so much, I felt almost shy of her when she did come home.

Lucien and I were only allowed short visits with Father. Those visits always made me nervous. Father was so weak and disoriented from loss of blood and medication that he hardly spoke and I didn't know what to say to him, but Mama said just seeing us there did Father good.

With Father in the hospital, and Lucien and I just trying to keep up with the work that needed doing, no one had given much thought to the new barn. No one, that is, except Uncle Sturgis.

One Saturday morning, just as Lucien and I had finished milking the cows in the yard and put them out to pasture, we saw trucks coming up the drive. Not just one truck, but more than a dozen. They all rolled into the yard, and I recognized Zeeb Wilson, Olin Marckres, Jervis Potter, Hilas Bumps, and most of our other neighbors. Right behind them, four big flatbed trucks ground their way up the hill, two of them loaded with beams and one each with lumber and steel roofing.

Uncle Sturgis swung out the door of Zeeb's truck and walked over to where Lucien and I were standing, dumbfounded.

"It's looking like we'll need a foreman here," he said to Lucien. "You look like a good candidate. What do we do, boss?"

"What's all this?" Lucien asked.

"We're building you a barn," Uncle Sturgis said. "You can't keep milking those cows outside forever. Lapoint's Sawmill had timber all cut for a barn out toward Eden, but the folks quit farming, so I got the timber cheap. With all these men here, you should have a frame up by nightfall."

Seeing as how Lucien was still standing there like a stunned steer, Uncle Sturgis began directing the flatbed trucks and setting men into position. I didn't know what to do.

"We got any food in the kitchen?" Lucien whispered to me. "Enough to feed this many?" I knew we didn't, but I didn't have to worry long.

A caravan of cars was following the trucks. All the women of the church tumbled out with pots, and pans, and covered dishes. Olin Marckres had brought some of the church tables in the back of his truck, and I helped the women set these up in the front yard. For once, I was glad to see Aunt Lurdine. She loved to organize things, and ordering people around was right down her alley. Before I knew it, the women had loaded those tables with enough food to feed twice the number there. There was every food imaginable: baked beans, potato and macaroni salads, chicken and biscuits, ham, flannel hash, tuna casseroles, graham rolls, and the dessert table looked like it might buckle under cookies and brownies and apple pandowdy, twelve different cakes, and pies of every flavor: apple, raspberry, blueberry, lemon meringue, rhubarb, mince and my favorite, gooseberry.

Mrs. Bumps handed me a jar of her homemade pickles.

"I brought these especially for you," she said.

I'd never been to a barn-raising before, and I was caught up in all the activity and excitement. We were going to have a new barn! True, it wouldn't be old and safe-feeling like our barn had been, at least not right off, but I was lonesome for any sort of a barn right now.

The men got busy laying out all the beams on the ground, sawing them to length and cutting and fitting the joints. All this was done on the ground, where it was easier to work. Even working hard, the men laughed and joked, and the noise melted in with the ringing of saws and hammers. I was kept busy, too, carrying tools from one place to another as they were needed, chisels and squares and tape measures.

Lucien barked at me several times to stay out of everybody's way, but when Uncle Sturgis saw how much I wanted to help, he set me down beside him and showed me how to cut a hole in one end of a beam so that the end of another beam could fit into it and be held together by a wooden peg. The hole was called a mortise and the piece that fit into it was called a tenon. Uncle Sturgis helped me cut a mortise with an old mortising drill that you had to crank by hand, then showed me how to make the hole rectangular with a chisel. After he was satisfied that I knew what I was doing, he set me to work drilling and chiseling out the mortises for a whole row of beams and my heart sang with each bite of the chisel and bit. I was helping to build us a new barn.

By noon, all the joints had been fashioned, and the bents put together, and the men broke off to eat. The morning's work had fueled already big appetites, and I was astonished to see the food disappear. I was afraid it would all be gone by the time I got to eat, but the women didn't let that happen. I filled up on ham, and turkey, and potato salad, and macaroni and cheese, and scalloped potatoes, and Mrs. Bumps's pickles, and finished off with two pieces of gooseberry pie. I ate faster than I should have, but I knew the men were getting ready to raise the bents to start building the frame of the barn and I didn't want to miss out on any of it.

Jervis Potter had helped raise lots of barns, so Lucien put him in charge of directing the raising. There were three men put at each upright beam, and several on the crossbeam, and on the count of three they all heaved and lifted the bent so that it angled upward. The men on the crossbeam pushed it up as far as they could, and then other men with long pike poles pushed the bent the rest of the way until it was standing in position, and the tenons on the vertical beams dropped down into the holes, or mortises, made to hold them. Then ash pegs were hammered into holes to hold the joints snug. I couldn't believe you could build a whole barn frame, one that didn't wiggle or shake, without a single nail.

There were five bents in all that had to be raised, and as each one went up, I grew more excited, seeing the barn lengthen and grow. In the morning it had seemed like nothing was happening, and I wondered if the barn frame would be up in a week, but by figuring and fitting everything on the ground, the raising itself went right quick.

Work on the second floor was slower, just by having to lift the beams with rope and tackle. The men laid down a temporary floor of old planks so they had a surface on which to work while they fit together the bents for the second floor. Lucien wouldn't let me climb a ladder to the second floor; he thought I'd be in the way, and I got madder at him when he gave me an errand.

"Iris," he said, "go up there behind the pond and cut down a small fir tree, one about half your size."

I figured he was just trying to get me out of the way, like you do to a little kid, and I resented it. What'd he want an old fir tree for, anyhow? It wasn't Christmas.

"You're just sending me up there to get me out of the way. You don't have to make up an excuse, like getting a stupid tree."

"No, I mean it," Lucien said, earnestly. "We'll need it, you'll see."

I still wasn't sure I believed him, so I was still grumpy, but I got the bucksaw from the toolshed and headed out beyond the pond. It was a beautiful day, not too hot and with a breeze blowing; we'd been lucky to get such fine weather for the raising.

I didn't go up to the softwoods on the ridge. I didn't want to be reminded of Father's accident right then, so I walked along the edge of the swamp until I came onto a bushy little fir as tall as my waist. Half my size, Lucien had said. It took only a couple of strokes with the saw to cut it down, and I swung the tree over my shoulder to carry it home.

Aunt Lurdine saw me coming, handed me a dishtowel and set me to work drying dishes. I'd been sick of fetching tools, but that was a sight more fun than drying dishes.

The sun was close to setting when the last rafter was put

in place and pegged. It had been a long day, and I knew the men must be tired, but they were folks used to long hours and hard work, and I could see the satisfaction in their faces when they looked at the barn frame.

"I'd say that's about it for one day, hey, Lucien?" Hilas Bumps called out. Lucien held up his hand.

"Just one more thing and it'll be finished," he said. "Iris, go fetch that tree."

When I'd brought him the tree, Lucien sent me up the series of ladders to the top floor, and followed right behind me, with the tree in one hand. He buckled his own belt around me, tucked a hammer in the belt, and handed me a couple of nails.

"Here, Iris," he said, "you're a good climber, and I know you're not afraid of heights. Think you can shinny up along that rafter there, all the way to the top? Once you're up there, I'll toss the tree to you and you nail it to the peak. It's a tradition; the tree is supposed to bring good luck and prosperity to the farm."

I shinnied up that rafter like I was a squirrel. I was a long way above the ground, but Lucien was right, I wasn't afraid of heights. In fact, I love them. I felt like I'd been born climbing, and I was doing an important job here. I sure hoped this tree would bring good luck. Seemed we could use some.

When I reached the very peak of the roof, and hooked a leg over the ridge to hoist myself on top, I heard a gasp in the crowd and then Aunt Lurdine's screechy voice.

"Iris Anderson, you come down from there this instant!"

"It's all right, Lurdine," Lucien hollered down to her. "I asked her to do it. She's the best climber here," and I felt proud as he said it.

I held on with my legs while I attached the tree. It was hard holding the tree with one hand and nailing it with the other, but I finally managed to get it in place, though I thought the first stiff breeze would probably take the tree sailing over into the next county. Not the barn frame, though. It felt solid and safe as a granite ledge beneath me.

I climbed back down beside Lucien and looked up to see the little tree.

"Don't that look grand," I heard Uncle Sturgis say, and it did.

Lucien shook the hand of every man as they left, and thanked them for their hard work. As they climbed into their trucks, Olin Marckres hollered, "We'll be back on Monday to put the roof on."

Uncle Sturgis was climbing into Zeeb's truck when Lucien gripped his shoulder.

"We can't pay you for this, Sturgis," Lucien said, quietly.

"You ain't supposed to," Uncle Sturgis said. "Your father's like a brother to me, and he's done things to help most of the men here. They all wanted to help."

Uncle Sturgis looked across the yard toward the barn frame and his eyes were shining.

"It looks good, doesn't it," he said. "Feels right to build something that'll last. I want that barn to endure long after I'm gone. Somedays I think farming's the only thing really worth doing."

I looked at him, surprised. I'd never imagined Uncle Sturgis felt that way about farming. I guess I'd always pictured him at work in the mill and never doing anything else.

"Did you grow up on a farm?" I asked him.

Uncle Sturgis nodded.

"I'd still be living on it, too, if my daddy hadn't been

killed in France in 1918. I tried to hold onto the farm for my mama, but we lost it anyway. It 'bout killed my mama, and me, too, having to leave that farm."

Uncle Sturgis kind of shook himself, and looked embarrassed. "Didn't mean to go on like that. It's just this farm means something to me, too, and I'm proud to help with the barn."

"Why don't you go into farming now?" I asked.

Uncle Sturgis looked over my head at Lucien.

"Well, you know Lurdine," he said. "Can you picture her a farmer's wife?" He shook his head, not waiting for an answer, and climbed into the truck.

The long line of cars and trucks snaked back down the bumpy road, and Lucien and I were left alone again, standing beside each other as we watched the bobbing taillights move back toward town. After all the noise of the day, the laughing, shouting, sawing, hammering and dishes rattling, it seemed strange to be wrapped in silence again as the darkness stole in on us. Strange, but comforting, too, and Lucien and I lingered in the yard a little longer, listening to the frogs call from the pond and grouse drum off in the woods. I felt tired yet more rested in my mind than I had in days. It was a glorious feeling to stand there and see the frame of our new barn straight and strong against the dying light. Seemed to me to be a promise of better times ahead. Maybe this would be enough to convince Lucien to come back to the farm.

"This'll be just the medicine Father needs to get better," Lucien said. "We'll drive up to the hospital tomorrow afternoon and tell him."

CHAPTER NINE

As Lucien and I entered the intensive care unit, Father turned his eyes toward us, eyes dulled by pain and medication. Each time I'd seen him since the accident, I was shocked anew that I could barely recognize him. It wasn't only that his face was gray and his eyes sunk into his head, or that he was hooked up to all those machines, but he looked a least twenty years older. I wanted to cry.

"Hi," he said in a voice that sounded like it belonged to someone else. I stared at him, and like before, I felt my throat constrict and no words came out.

Lucien told him about the barn-raising and I saw tears form in Father's eyes.

"Such good people," he whispered. "Such good neighbors."

I wanted to tell him about cutting the mortises and about putting the tree at the top of the roof, and how it had felt to be a part of that whole wonderful event, but Father closed his eyes and lay quiet and I didn't dare disturb him. I wondered if he'd drifted off to sleep, but then his lips moved.

"Think you can handle haying?" he whispered to Lucien.

"Iris and I can handle it just fine," Lucien said, and I felt proud he'd included me. Father opened one eye to study me.

"That all right with you?" he said and I nodded dumbly. I practically ran from the hospital when Lucien and I left, and once outside, I stood in the parking lot gulping great breaths of air.

With all that was happening, I didn't even feel my usual joy when school finished up and summer began. The last half of June was hot, the grass grew lush and beautiful, and Lucien and I started haying. The wild roses were in full bloom, circling the fields like a necklace and edging the roads with fragrant blossoms. The smell of roses was so sweet and thick I could have spooned it from the air.

I loved wild roses. I'd thought often about having sisters, all of us with wildflower names: Iris, Rose, Violet, Lily, and Daisy. (Ferris had named my imaginary brothers Toadflax and Stinking Benjamin.) But as much as I loved wild roses, I hardly had time to enjoy them. There was too much work for Lucien and me what with Mama being at the hospital most of the time. We were up before dawn to do the milking, then Lucien would head out to the fields to mow while I washed the milking machines and cleaned the gutters, then I would join him in the field to help with the raking and baling.

Before the summer, I hadn't had much experience with either. I'd driven the tractor plenty, but Lucien or Father had always done the mowing, raking and baling, but this summer we just didn't have a choice. The house was a mess, what with us just grabbing meals on the run and bolting for the barn or fields, and when Mama did come home, she was mostly cleaning up behind us. But she stayed home more when we were getting the hay in the barn and drove the tractor while Lucien and I loaded the wagons. Some days, Ferris came over to help us and Lucien tossed the bales up onto the wagon while Ferris and I stacked them. Lucien showed us how to tie in a load, crisscrossing every other tier of bales so the load would hold tight on the bumpy drive back to the barn. Those rides were the only time we got to rest between loads, and I'd lie back on the hay, watching the clouds and hawks sail by. It was always a relief to get a load, but every time we were in the barn, I wished we were back out in the field. The barn was like an oven under its new steel roof, and chaff stuck to my sweaty skin and itched all over like a thousand biting mosquitoes.

Uncle Sturgis took a few days off from work to help us, too. Said he enjoyed getting outdoors and doing some real work for a change. He stayed late those nights, helping us get the last bales in, and then helping us milk. He told jokes and stories and seemed reluctant to leave us to go back home. But I'd have been reluctant to leave, too, if I had to go home to Aunt Lurdine.

Most nights, after the last load was in, we'd head down to the pond for a dip before going home to do chores. After a day of sweating and itching, nothing felt so good as that cold, dark water.

I was glad, too, when Sundays came, because we couldn't hay on Sunday. Our church was firm for keeping the Sabbath day holy, which meant other than milking, no work was to be done, no haying, no sugaring, no chopping corn, and no woodcutting. When they'd gotten married, Mama had made Father promise he wouldn't work on Sunday. Father always worked so hard that Mama declared he wouldn't be alive now if he hadn't had that one day of rest a week. And while I chafed through the long sermon, hating to dress up and having to sit so still, I liked the day off from farmwork, too.

Most Sundays, nothing much happened. Father would fall asleep on the couch, listening to the ballgame on the radio. We couldn't fish or play cards on Sunday, but we could read, or walk in the woods, or take family drives. What I liked best was when we all piled in the car, drove over to Stone Pond, and spent the afternoon swimming. Father was a good swimmer, and he always swam across the pond and back first thing, but once back with us, he'd balance us on his hands and throw us out over the water. I felt like a kingfisher then, poised above the pond for an instant and then plunging down into the water. Other times, in the fall, we'd drive over by Wheeler Mountain, exploring the back roads and seeing the colors sweep over the hills like a forest fire.

I spent a lot of my time worrying, wondering if we'd ever do those things together as a family again. I woke up screaming some nights, having dreamed Father was dead. I thought how lonely and boring it would be to lay in the hospital day after day, so each time I visited Father I took him something. I tried to pick items I thought he'd like and would remind him of good times: things to touch like a baseball or a smooth stone from the brook, and things to smell like wild roses and a branch of balsam that brought the fragrance of outdoors into his stale, medicinal room. He always thanked me, but nothing I took him ever brought a sparkle to his eyes like I hoped it would. I wondered how much longer Father would have to stay at the hospital.

We were working on the last hayfield one hot day, just Lucien and me, when I saw Lucien glance up and stiffen. I looked to see what he was watching.

Mama was walking across the field, slowly, her head down, and a chill passed over me like a cloud blotting out the sun. She'd been at the hospital all afternoon, and I knew, looking at her, that something had changed.

She walked right up to us without saying a word.

"Is Father dead?" I whispered.

Mama sighed.

"No," she said slowly. "No, he's not dead. But they had to take the leg."

For a moment, I was sure even the bees and cicadas stopped to listen. I stood stupidly, wondering where they'd taken Father's leg. Then I saw the look on Lucien's face and I knew what she meant.

I turned and threw up in the grass.

CHAPTER TEN

Ferris came over two days later. Seemed like all she'd been doing all spring was offering me emotional support, and I ached for the times back when things hadn't been so weighty between us, when we'd just worried about our grades, or what our friends said, or how we were going to split a nickel's worth of candy. I was so tired of feeling sad all the time, and tired of worrying about what would hit us next.

"How much longer is your father going to be in the hospital?" Ferris asked. She was careful not to say anything about his leg.

"They're fitting him with an artificial leg," I told her.

Since I'd brought it up, she figured it was okay to talk about it.

"You mean a wooden leg?" I knew she'd read *Treasure Island*, too.

"No, they're not made of wood, anymore. It's mostly metal, I think, with straps to hold it on." I hadn't seen the leg yet, but Mama had told me a little about it. I didn't want to talk about it anyway. Ferris sensed that and didn't ask any more questions. But I wondered: how would Father run the farm with just one leg? Would Lucien leave again soon?

In July, after the first crop of hay was in, Aunt Lurdine thought it would be a great idea if she started a 4-H group. Right off, I knew it would mean trouble. I would have liked 4-H if we'd been able to do a horse project, or raise sheep, or plant trees for conservation, but Aunt Lurdine had other plans. She thought it was high time to shape the local girls into ladies, to teach the art of refinement and get back to the basics of cooking and sewing.

"I'm not going," I said to Mama when she told me. "I hate that stuff."

Mama looked worried. "How would it look, Iris, if she started that group, and her own niece didn't show up? It would make Aunt Lurdine feel bad."

"I don't care," I shouted. "She makes *me* feel bad a lot."

"Now, Iris, I want you to go. You need something to get your mind off your father. If you go into this group with an open mind, you might enjoy it." Why did mothers always say that? How could she possibly think I'd enjoy cooking and sewing, two things I'd always hated, taught by someone I'd always hated? But though I ranted and railed against it, Mama made me go.

There were five of us at that first meeting: Ferris (her mother had made her go, too), Amelia Marckres, and two of the Wilson girls, Jennie and Caroline. Ferris wasn't any happier to be there than I was, but I was glad she was there for moral support.

Aunt Lurdine opened the meeting by making us learn the 4-H creed, then she made us sing a dumb song, and then she explained that the purpose of our group was to become better citizens, improve our community and to learn skills that would make us good wives and mothers.

Ferris and I rolled our eyes at each other. I wouldn't mind doing something for the community, but I didn't want anything to do with that wife and mother junk. Then Aunt Lurdine told us the first thing we'd be working on. We were supposed to grow our fingernails as a personal hygiene project. What did fingernails have to do with betterment of the community, for gosh sakes?

"Now, don't be discouraged at how they look right now," Aunt Lurdine said. "It takes hard work and patience, but in six weeks, your nails will be long and beautiful." There was a whole page in our booklet, telling how to have beautiful fingernails: always wash with warm water, eat gelatin to strengthen them, and each night, gently push, never cut, the cuticle down to the base of the nail.

"This is the dumbest thing I ever read," Ferris whispered, and I had to agree.

"At the end of six weeks," Aunt Lurdine said, "we'll compare fingernails and give a prize to the winner."

I'd already decided I wouldn't do it. For the next six weeks, I knew I wouldn't push a cuticle, and neither would Ferris. I'd never win anyway, and it wasn't even a contest I wanted to win. Amelia or Jennie would be the ones to win a stupid contest like that. I figured I might as well just keep chewing my nails and avoid all the hassle.

At each meeting, Aunt Lurdine took roll call as if she couldn't see all five of us with her bare eyes. And she wouldn't just call our first names; she had to roll the whole name off her tongue.

"Iris Huldah Anderson?" she'd say.

I could have slapped her, calling out that middle name I hated so. Every time, one or two of the girls giggled. And why not? Whoever heard of such an ugly name as Huldah?

It was a word I'd expect to see in one of the *National Geographic* magazines that Ferris's mother stored in their attic. It seemed like something you'd read in a caption, like "The aborigines of Australia live in buildings called huldahs."

After one meeting, when Mama picked me up and we were riding home, I remarked bitterly about having such a wretched name.

"You were named after your great-aunt Huldah," Mama told me, as if that made any difference. "She's a great lady, you know. She's a missionary in Pakistan."

"I know, Mama," I said, rolling my eyes. "But it still doesn't make it a good name. Iris isn't great, either, for that matter. Why couldn't you name me something normal?"

"I don't understand you," Mama said. "Iris are such beautiful flowers."

"Sure," I said, "but it's an ugly name. And besides, I'm not even pretty."

"What do you mean?" Mama cried. "You are pretty." But mothers have to say things like that. I hadn't meant to bring it up. I hardly ever thought about being pretty or not, probably because I knew I wasn't, so why make it an issue?

Another project Aunt Lurdine dreamed up to torture us was for us to prepare a meal for the rest of the group. Aunt Lurdine did say we could work in groups of two. Since there were five of us, Ferris and I quickly said we'd team up, and the other three could work together. That made the teams pretty lopsided. Amelia, Jennie, and Caroline all liked to cook and could probably whip up a seven-course gourmet meal, while Ferris and I would be doing well if we just didn't poison anyone. Aunt Lurdine said we should have our menu planned for the next meeting.

"And," she said, "I want everyone to be thinking what we should call our group. We have to have a name." I was going to suggest "Lurdine's Slaves," but I kept my mouth shut.

The night before our next meeting, Mama collared Ferris and me in the kitchen.

"I know you two have to present a menu tomorrow. Don't you think you should start planning it?" She put her cookbook in front of us.

"I'll leave you two to figure it out," she said. "I'm going to rest." Mama always seemed tired these days.

Ferris and I couldn't think of anything to serve.

"It's got to be easy," I said, "so we don't have to spend much time making it."

"How about peanut butter and jelly sandwiches?" Ferris suggested.

"Naw, Aunt Lurdine would never allow it. We probably have to cook something."

"Grilled cheese sandwiches?" Ferris said, hopefully.

That might work. "Maybe," I said, "as long as we have something else to go with them."

"How about some pudding for dessert?"

"Good. See if we have any."

Ferris pawed through the cupboard and came up with three boxes of pudding: chocolate, butterscotch, and lemon.

"Good," I said again. "We'll just mix 'em together."

Ferris had found a bag of marshmallows, too, and she was reading something on the package.

"Listen to this," she said. "Here's a recipe for pineapple, green peppers, marshmallows, and tuna, all put together."

I made gagging noises.

"Quick, get rid of that recipe before Aunt Lurdine sees it, or we'll get that salad on Thanksgiving."

Ferris ignored me and continued to read.

"It says for best enjoyment, add mayonnaise just before serving."

I reached for the bag. "For best enjoyment, I'm getting rid of that recipe."

"No, wait," said Ferris. "Let's serve it at our dinner."

The more we thought about it, the more awful dishes we came up with. Maybe putting on this supper wouldn't be so bad after all.

Mama came in a while later.

"Have you two planned your menu yet?" We nodded, trying to keep straight faces.

"Yes, Mama. We're going to have a salad and pudding for dessert." I didn't tell her we'd planned on adding chicken liver to the pudding.

"And cake," I said. Ferris stared at me. That was news to her.

"Sounds like an unusual supper," Mama said.

When she was out of the room again, Ferris cornered me.

"What kind of cake?" she wanted to know.

"Just cake," I said, giggling.

"What's funny about that?" she asked.

"You'll see," I said, as mysteriously as I could.

We put that supper on, a week later. Sitting on Aunt Lurdine's table, in Mama's prettiest dishes, even I had to admit the food *looked* delicious, though I knew it would gag a pig. The other girls were surprised, too, though they sniffed suspiciously at the pudding. Aunt Lurdine clapped her hands and beamed when I carried in the cake.

"How lovely!" she cried. "This group has done wonders for you girls," she said, meaning me and Ferris.

It was a beautiful cake, in the shape of a rabbit, covered

with white frosting. Around the cake, I had arranged black jelly beans.

"What are those, dear?" Aunt Lurdine asked, sweetly.

"Rabbit turds," I hollered gleefully, breaking into peals of laughter. I hadn't had so much fun all summer. And it was even more satisfying to watch Aunt Lurdine's face turn three shades of purple.

After that, no one took a bite of our food, and Aunt Lurdine sent us home early. I was disappointed. I'd wanted to see Aunt Lurdine's face when she tasted that pudding. We'd sweetened it with red pepper.

CHAPTER ELEVEN

I was sitting on the porch, tears streaming down my face when Ferris biked over.

"What's the matter with you?" she asked, and her face paled. "Is it your father?"

"Naw, just horseradish," I said, and scraped the last little piece of horseradish root against Mama's tin grater, catching my knuckles and adding just a little skin into the ground-up horseradish. I loved horseradish, soaked as it was in vinegar, but grating it was no fun. It made your eyes water worse than onions did, and the roots were so hard it took a long time to grate.

Ferris sat down next to me.

"How is your father?" she asked.

"Okay, I guess. He's coming home tomorrow."

Ferris just nodded her head. I was glad she didn't say anything, like "That's great," because truth is, I wasn't sure how I felt about it. Part of me wanted Father home, and part of me was scared to have him around. He didn't seem like Father in the hospital, but maybe he'd be his old self once he got home. I was afraid of how he'd changed, what I'd say to him, how I'd act around him. But maybe, when he came home, things around the farm would finally start getting back to normal.

"I'm done," I said, standing up. "Let's go get some green apples."

I loved green apples, too, and I always laughed when folks told me I'd get a bellyache if I ate too many. I'd eaten hundreds over the years and never had a bellyache, not once. That story seemed as stupid as having to wait an hour after we ate before we could go swimming.

Ferris and I filled our pockets with green apples and ate them in the pasture. We bit off a little piece of apple to expose the juicy white flesh and then rubbed that part on the salt block so the juice would dissolve some of the salt and pick up the flavor. It didn't bother us that heifers had licked the salt block all over. Green apples just weren't the same without salt.

We finished the apples and wondered what to do next.

"Let's go see if the showy lady's slippers have blossomed yet," I said, leading her into the swamp.

The air was still and cool under the canopy of leaves. A few warblers called, and we heard the *rat-tat-tat* of a woodpecker. Under our feet, the ground seemed so spongy I was tempted to take off my sneakers so I could wiggle my toes in the moss, but I watched where I stepped because Lucien had showed me several rare orchids that grew in the swamp. I felt like I'd entered a magical kingdom.

"Isn't it beautiful in here?" I whispered.

"What's so great about it?" Ferris answered. "It's just a swamp," but I saw the glint of sunlight on lady's slippers and ferns and heard the whir of ducks startled from water. To me it was beautiful.

When we got back and Ferris left for home, I went into

the kitchen for a drink of water. I got a glass from the drainer by the sink, and was about to open the fridge when I heard voices coming from the living room. I peeked through the doorway and saw Lucien and Mama sitting on the couch. Mama looked upset and something in the tone of their voices made me stop and listen.

"What did Father say?" Lucien said.

"Your father's terribly depressed," Mama said. "Says he can't run a farm with just one leg. Says he can't do much of anything, now that he's a cripple." Mama's voice had tears in it. "I tried to tell him everything would be all right, that we'd manage, but he thinks his life is over. He'll be coming home tomorrow and I don't know what to do." I'd never heard Mama sound so hopeless before.

I slept fitfully that night, worrying and wondering what would happen when Father came home. How would he act? And would he be able to do the things around the farm that he had before?

At one point during the night, I heard Mama moving around downstairs. Was Mama nervous, too, about tomorrow's homecoming?

In the morning, I told Mama I'd clean the house and have lunch made for when they got back, so while Lucien and Mama went to pick up Father at the hospital, I swept and mopped the floors, made egg salad and olive sandwiches, washed the dishes and lettered a sign that said "Welcome home, Father. We love you." to hang on the door. Then I waited nervously for them to return.

I heard the car in the driveway and ran to open the screen door for them. Lucien and Mama helped Father into the house, brushing past me to get him settled on the couch. Father didn't mention the sign on the door. He sat down heavily and sighed. I tried not to stare where his leg used to be.

"Well, home at last," Mama said cheerfully.

When she got no response, I offered what I'd been thinking.

"You haven't seen the new barn, Father. I thought I could show it to you."

Before Father could answer, Mama jumped in.

"That's a wonderful idea, Iris. Doesn't that sound fun, Hazen?"

I squirmed uncomfortably. Mama was talking to Father as if he was two years old.

"Maybe later," Father said without a trace of enthusiasm.

A frown crossed Mama's face, but by the time she turned to me, she was all smiles again, cheerfulness ringing false in her voice.

"I'm sure he'll want to as soon as he rests up some," she said. "Goodness, he just got home from the hospital," like we didn't know that.

"Can I get you anything, Hazen?" she asked. Father shook his head, and Mama lowered her voice.

"Now, if you need to, you know, go to the bathroom or anything, you let Lucien or me know, and we'll help you."

I saw the muscles working in Father's jaw.

"For God's sake, Edith, quit treating me like a child," he said. "I do know how to go to the bathroom by myself."

Mama blinked, stung by his words.

"You're right," she said in her normal voice. "I'm sorry. I was just trying to help."

After that, we tiptoed around Father. I was afraid of him; he wasn't Father anymore. It wasn't just that he looked different being so thin and pale, but he was different inside. I felt like my Father had left and been replaced by this silent, angry man who snapped at us if we tried to do things for him, or worse, went for long stretches without saying a word. He'd been fitted with an artificial leg at the hospital, a big, clunky thing made of steel and leather, and Mama kept encouraging him to get outside, walk around, get used to it, but he'd snap at her, too, and just sit in the living room, staring at the floor.

Mama tried to sound cheerful, and reassured us that Father just needed some time and he'd get over it, but even I could hear the doubt in her voice.

"Uncle Armour, my great-uncle actually, lost a leg in World War I," Mama told me. "He was never the same afterward, but that had more to do with the horrors he'd seen, I imagine, than with losing his leg."

"What did Uncle Armour look like?"

"Goodness, I must have a photo of him someplace. Probably up in that big trunk in the attic."

I found the box of photographs up there, brown and faded images of the past, and something else, too, a small painting tucked underneath an old quilt. It showed wildflowers in a field with a line of mountains beyond, like the view from Beech Hill. I liked it, and carried it downstairs to show Mama.

"Your father painted that," Mama said proudly.

"He did?" Mama nodded.

"I bet you didn't know that he played drums in a band, too, every Friday night," Mama said, staring off over my head, her voice dreamy. "And what a dancer."

"That's over," Father said, bitterly.

Mama sighed. "Maybe you could take up painting again, Hazen. You were really quite good."

"Oh, find something for the cripple to do, huh?"

"I didn't mean that," Mama cried. She was close to tears. Why did he have to snap at her like that?

I was angry at Father, but then I felt guilty for being angry at him. Some days, I'd close my eyes and imagine what it would be like if I opened them and one of my legs was missing. Gone. Yet even when I was pretending, I knew I couldn't really know what Father was going through 'cause when he shut his eyes and opened them, the leg was still gone.

I wondered if Father had done that, closed his eyes and then opened them, hoping his leg would be there when he looked. Knowing it wasn't and yet, just hoping it had all been a nightmare, a terrible mistake, and the leg was back. And then seeing the stump, and knowing it was truly gone, and his body, and his life, would never be the same again. My strong father who once could work from sunup to sundown without tiring now couldn't even get dressed without help. I figured I'd be mad, too, and lash out, just like Father did.

One day, Lucien took Father out to show him around the new barn. They hadn't been gone long when the screen door banged open, and Lucien came in, half-supporting, half-carrying Father. Mama's face drained of color, and I realized then she'd been afraid ever since Father came home of letting him out of her sight.

"What happened?" she said.

"He's all right, Mama, just a bump on the head," Lucien said, helping Father to the couch. "He just tried to climb up on the tractor, slipped and fell."

"Why would you do that, Hazen?" Mama asked.

"To see if I could do one thing again like I used to,"

Father said. He spit the words out like nails. "To see if I could be of any use around here again. I guess I got my answer," he added bitterly.

"If you'd just give yourself some time," Mama said.

Father shook his head.

"Time won't give me back my leg. I've made a decision. I'm selling the farm."

Mama, Lucien, and I stood as still as stumps. It was like someone had twisted a knife in my belly.

"What?" Mama said. She looked bewildered. We all did. "But why?"

"I can't run the farm now," Father said. "That should be obvious."

"But Lucien's here now," Mama said. None of us had moved.

"Yes," said Father, his voice still bitter. "We have him chained here like a dog. He doesn't want to be here. And why should he? Taking care of a crippled old man. When I was in the hospital, Sturgis offered me a job. They're opening up a new furniture plant, and he wants me to run it."

"But . . ." Mama began.

"No buts," Father shouted. "I've made my decision." Father had never raised his voice to Mama.

Mama stared steadily at Father for the longest time. Then she drew herself up to her full height, and I thought she was going to let him have it.

"All right, Hazen. If you think it best."

And as simple as that, in less than five minutes, we'd lost our farm. In less than five minutes, my whole life had turned upside down. My stomach churned, and I knew I was going to be sick.

Lucien studied Mama and Father for a moment and went outside without saying a word.

Still staring at Father, Mama said quietly, "Iris, please go upstairs."

Without saying a word, I did as Mama said. I closed the door behind me, and I really meant to obey and go upstairs, but I knew my only hope for the farm lay with Mama. She may have sounded like she'd let the matter drop, but that was just for Lucien's and my benefit.

"Edith, I don't want to discuss this," I heard Father say.

"Shh," Mama said. "Wait till Iris gets upstairs."

I knew they were listening for me, so I climbed two of the steps, exaggerating the loudness of my footfalls, then stood on one step, and stomped my feet loudly to sound like I was ascending the stairs, then held still after what I guessed was the right number of stairsteps. Then I crept down the stairs like a ghost and crouched on the bottom step to listen to Mama and Father. They almost never argued, but they were arguing now.

"Why, Hazen? We've put our life's blood into this farm. Why are you selling it?"

"Are you blind, woman? It's hard enough running a farm with two good legs, and I'm one short."

"We've been through hard times before. I've never seen you give up."

"I'm tired of always being in debt, Edith. Maybe with that new job I can get ahead a little, give you things you deserve. I want a better life for Lucien and Iris, but especially for you."

"You fool, Hazen. Don't you know I've had the life I've wanted right here with you."

"But, Lurdine said you've missed out on the finer things in life, things Sturgis has been able to give her."

"Sometimes, Lurdine doesn't know spit," Mama said, angrily. I knew her eyes were flashing. "Sturgis is sweet, and he's been a wonderful husband to Lurdine, but he's not half the man you are. I can't think of a finer thing to be in all the world than a farmer."

"I used to take a lot of pride in that," Father said wearily. "But look at me, now. I need you, or Lucien, to help me around, to help do just about everything around here."

"You're still a farmer, Hazen. You know as well as anyone farming's not a job, it's who you are. It takes over your life, but you always said it's what you wanted. And if you used the eyes in your head, you'd know that's what Iris wants, too."

There was a moment's silence before Father went on.

"She's a long way off from deciding that. She's only thirteen. She could change her mind. I don't want her to be chained here like Lucien's been."

"But if you sell the farm, she'll never have the choice. I know most kids can't wait to get off into the world, but I think she'll stay. Iris feels things more deeply than most people. She loves this farm; its a part of her, and I don't think she'll feel differently when she's older."

That surprised me. All along, I'd been feeling that Mama didn't understand me, and here she was explaining my feelings to Father in a way that showed she knew me.

"Edith, we're the ones who don't have a choice. Money was tight to begin with and the hospital bills will put us in debt for a long time. We can't wait for something in the future we're not even sure will happen. We've got to sell," and my heart sank when Mama didn't answer.

Mama called me downstairs later to go help Lucien with chores. She didn't say anything about her talk with Father. I felt wooden and numb. Everything bad that could happen had happened and all to me. Grandpa dead, Father crippled and now having to sell the farm. Maybe God was punishing me for being mad at him, but that seemed a mean trick. All that stuff Mama had been feeding me for years, like God is good, God is love, was all lies and God had it in for me. He was in cahoots with Aunt Lurdine to make my life miserable.

I finished up chores and carried a jug of milk to the house. I was just about to open the screen door when I saw something that twisted my heart.

CHAPTER TWELVE

Mama was bending over the sink, peeling potatoes and bawling. The tears dripped off the end of her nose onto the ribs of peel piled on the edge of the sink. It about tore me apart to see my strong mother crying. She'd had a year of heartache, too; she'd lost a father, near lost a husband, and now was losing her farm, and we were all leaning on her for strength and comfort, but I didn't see that she had anyone to lean on.

I should have run to her, thrown my arms around her, tried to comfort her. I should have, but I didn't. Mama thought she was alone, and would be embarrassed by her tears. I snuck back to the barn and came back in later with Lucien. Mama was all composed now. Her eyes were still red, but she wore her brave smile for us and talked to us through supper with a false note of gaiety in her voice.

"It will be hard for awhile," she said, "but I'm sure we'll all adjust soon. The new furniture mill is opening up in White River Junction and I imagine I'll be able to get a job as clerk in one of the stores down there."

White River Junction. I couldn't believe my ears. White

River Junction was more than a hundred miles south, near the New Hampshire border.

"I thought the mill would be close by," I said. "If we had to move, I figured it'd at least be Craftsbury or Glover."

"I'm afraid not, honey."

White River Junction. It might as well be the moon.

Mama was watching me.

"Oh, honey, I know it's going to be hard. We just have to trust in the Lord."

"How can you say that?" I cried. "I prayed for Father's leg to be saved, and he lost it, didn't he? God didn't answer my prayers, and he didn't answer yours, either."

"Oh, Iris," Mama said, tiredly. "God always answers our prayers. It's just that sometimes the answer is no. And he did answer my prayers. Father's alive, isn't he?"

I lay awake most of the night, wanting to scream, to cry, to curl up in a ball and never get up. With just a few words, my whole life had turned upside down. Even when everything else in my life was falling apart, Grandpa, Father, the barn burning, I'd always known I'd have the fields and woods to run to, a place, like Gilead, to find solace. I couldn't believe, didn't want to believe, that someone could take it all away from me.

There had to be something I could do. Maybe if I earned some money, I could give it to Father and he wouldn't feel he had to sell the farm. Lucien had said the raspberries were ripe on the east side of Beech Hill. Maybe I could sell berries to the store in town.

Mama and Father had a meeting at the bank, so Lucien and I ate breakfast alone.

"Do you think Mr. Wylie would buy some raspberries?" I asked him. I didn't say anything about using the money to save the farm, but my stomach churned every time I thought about it.

"Don't see why not," Lucien said. "When I get back this afternoon, I'll run your berries into town."

I buckled one of Lucien's belts around my waist and through the handles of three lard pails. Having the pails hanging around my waist freed up my hands for picking. In good picking, I could fill a pail in about an hour, depending on how many I ate. When I picked with Mama, she made me chew gum to keep my mouth busy so I wouldn't stuff it full of berries she wanted for pies and jam. Being alone today, I left the gum at home.

I whistled to Gretel, and she raced ahead of me across the fields and up the cowpath to the top of Beech Hill. I stood there a few minutes looking toward the Green Mountains. The day was turning hot, but up here, the wind was cool and as I faced it, I felt a bit calmer.

I headed down the other side of the hill, down into what had been Grandpa's sugar bush. It was called Beech Hill, but there were as many maples up here as beech trees, and there'd been even more until the 1938 hurricane had toppled the maples like matchsticks and raspberries had grown up to reclaim the land. Grandpa had cut a million board feet of lumber that year. I didn't know how much a million board feet was, but I knew it was a lot. Mama had told us a lot of stories about the black 1940 Ford Grandpa had bought with the earnings from that lumber, the first new car Grandpa had ever owned.

The raspberries hung round and plump as beads. I'd put on a long-sleeved shirt and jeans so I'd be protected against the thorns, and I plunged into the bushes, picking with both hands. I heard a rustling ahead of me and grinned.

Must be Gretel. She liked berries, too; I'd often seen her laying under a bush, daintily eating raspberries. I popped a berry in my mouth and heard Gretel barking, faintly, probably at a squirrel. She was still back on top of the hill.

A bear rose from the bushes, not ten feet from me. He squinted his little eyes and wrinkled his nose, trying to catch my scent. There were mashed berries sticking to his black fur.

I stood still as a stone. My heart was racing, partly from fear but more from excitement. I was thrilled to be this close to a bear. I'd seen their tracks on Beech Hill and had even seen one up here before, far away and just for a moment. But I'd never been this close to one before. I didn't say anything, I didn't move. I didn't know what the bear was going to do, and the thought flashed through my mind that Lucien might find me, or what was left of me, later this evening, but I had a deeper feeling, a stronger feeling, that the bear would not hurt me, and I was going to be all right.

The bear stared back at me for what seemed like a hundred minutes, then he dropped to all fours. He stared at me again, then turned his heavy body and disappeared in the bushes. I could hear him as he worked his way through the patch and out the other side, headed for the thick stand of spruce and fir to the north. As the sounds of his movement died away, my knees started shaking so bad I had to sit down to keep from falling. My heart was still racing, and I felt light-headed. What a story I had to tell, to Lucien, Mama, and Ferris. Mama probably wouldn't believe that I'd been more excited than afraid, but Ferris would. And Lucien, too. Lucien would understand.

When my knees, and hands, too, stopped shaking, I picked the three lard pails full of berries as quick as I could and almost ran back home. I picked the berries over, pulling out leaves, twigs and stinkbugs, and piled them in baskets, ready for Lucien to take to Mr. Wylie.

Lucien didn't come home till after dark. By that time, the store was closed, and my berries had settled and mashed together in their baskets. All that work for nothing.

Lucien sat down heavily in Father's chair, sighed and closed his eyes. He looked so tired.

I meant to be kind to him. He'd been working so hard, and he hadn't meant to forget about the raspberries. I wouldn't even remind him about them.

While Lucien ate a sandwich, I took the berries to the pantry. I found Mama's old cookbook, the binding torn and the covers bulging from all the recipes she'd cut out and saved, and managed to stir up a batch of baking powder biscuits. I put them in the oven, and went back out to the kitchen.

Lucien had finished his sandwich and was pushing his chair from the table.

"If you wait a few minutes," I said, "there'll be some raspberry shortcake ready," Lucien looked up, surprised.

"You made it?" he said.

"Don't get used to it," I told him. "Cooking ain't something I'm even going to spend much time practicing." Lucien smiled at me, remembering the 4-H group.

"We're all doing things we never expected to," he said, more to himself than to me.

Talking with Lucien, this way, seeing him relax after having to deal with everything since Father went into the hospital, I was glad I'd decided to forgive him for forgetting about the berries. I was glad until Lucien opened his mouth again.

"Maybe everything will turn out for the best when we don't have the farm anymore. It will be easier for all of us."

Bitterness, hot as fresh syrup, washed away my forgiveness.

"You could come back," I said, my voice sharp as a razor. "We could keep the farm if you came back."

I caught Lucien off-guard. He'd prepared himself to face Father and Mama, but I don't think he'd even considered how I might feel toward him. I wanted to wound him, wanted him to feel as badly as I did. But any fool, looking at his face, could tell he did.

"Yes," he said slowly. "I could. But would you really want me to spend the rest of my life doing something I didn't want to do?"

Yes, my inner voice raged. If it meant saving the farm. But I couldn't say that out loud to his eyes.

"Maybe you'd learn to like it," I said, half a question, half a plea, trying to convince myself more than him.

Lucien looked at me for over a minute before he spoke.

"You don't know what it was like," he said quietly. "Father angry all the time, always overworked, always in debt. Shoveling out the gutters which usually took all morning, then having it all start again the next day. Sitting on a cold tractor seat to spread manure, even when it was twenty or thirty below zero out there. Chopping frozen sawdust out of the silo in the dark. Milking, having cows slap me across the face with tails full of manure. Couldn't go out with . . ." He stopped, then continued on a different track, but I was pretty sure he'd been about to say Jeannine Hammett, a girl in his class that he'd had his eye on. She'd gotten married last summer.

"Ever since I can remember, I've wanted to be a writer.

The hardest thing I've ever done was to tell Father that I was going to college to study writing. Father always talked about me taking over the farm, doing all this for me. I knew I was crushing his dream. But I had to do it. And now you want me to give it all up again."

I couldn't answer him because I didn't understand. The farm meant everything to me, it was my dream of the future. How could it not mean the same to him?

CHAPTER THIRTEEN

Mama knew I was upset and angry and tried her best to cheer me up. What Mama didn't know was that I'd decided I wouldn't be moving with them. I'd made up my mind to run away and live in the woods.

When Mama wasn't looking, I began to squirrel things away, things I knew I'd need later to take care of myself. But I had to be careful. If I took too many things, or anything large, she'd miss them and might get suspicious, so I tried to pick items she wouldn't notice were gone. I figured whatever else I needed, I'd either have to make it or just do without.

"Now, where's my frying pan walked off to?" Mama asked one night before supper just as I was heading out to the barn to do chores.

Blood pounded in my ears. Maybe if I pretended I hadn't heard her, Mama wouldn't ask me directly. I hated to lie to Mama.

Mama went into the pantry to look for her pan and I sighed with relief, but my stomach still felt jittery. Keeping secrets was hard and the one about Draper was the biggest secret I'd ever kept. If Draper didn't admit to setting the fire soon, I was going to be a wreck.

Resentment toward my cousin flooded my stomach, replacing the jitters. I wondered if he was suffering *any* consequences from what he'd done, carried any guilt, but I doubted it. He'd probably forgotten all about it, while my life was being ruined by it.

I wanted to laugh and talk and forget for even a short time that we were losing the farm, so on the night before the auction, I invited Ferris to sleep out with me on Beech Hill.

We took two of her father's old army sleeping bags, a flashlight, some bread, gooseberry jam, and a mayonnaise jar of water. I made Ferris carry most of the gear because my hands were full with a bulging grain bag I slung over my shoulder. When we were safely out of sight of the house, I showed Ferris the contents of the grain sack: pots, the frying pan, spoons, rope, matches, a metal cup, and a spatula.

"What're you doing with all that stuff?" she wanted to know.

"I'm gonna hide it up by the old cellar-hole."

"What for?"

" 'Cause I'm not moving away," I told her. "I'm going to hide when they move and live up here in the woods."

I'd expected Ferris to be happy, knowing she wasn't going to lose her best friend, so I was disappointed to see the skeptical look on her face.

"Your parents won't leave without you," she said.

"Well, if they can't find me, maybe they'll decide to stay after all."

Ferris still looked doubtful.

"I don't think it will work," she said, and irritation toward her nibbled at my stomach. Why couldn't she be supportive of my decision? Whose side was she on, anyway?

We hiked to the top of Beech Hill to the spot where deer had lain and flattened the grass. We spread the sleeping bags there, crawled into them, and talked as the evening light faded and fireflies flickered through the twilight.

"Look! A falling star," I said, but by the time I'd pointed, the star had burned back into the darkness.

"I never see as many as you do," Ferris grumbled.

We talked about sports and books and animals, everything but the farm and Father.

"If you could come back as anything, what would it be?" I asked. Ferris thought a moment.

"A wild horse, I think," she said. "How 'bout you?"

That was easy. A bird of some kind, a hawk maybe, and I'd live my whole life up here on Beech Hill.

"I'm getting sleepy," Ferris mumbled. She always petered out first. "You tired?"

"Nope," I said. "I'm going to watch till I've counted fifty."

Ferris groaned. "I can't stay awake that long," she said, "but you will." Another reference to my stubbornness.

I lay still and stared up into the great bowl of sky. The best way to watch for meteors was to stare straight overhead and keep your eyes all soft to take in as much of the sky as possible. That way, even the falling stars out on the horizon caught your eyes, too. By the time I'd counted seventeen falling stars, I heard Ferris's soft snoring.

Then the sky began to change. At first there was just a milky light stretching across the northern horizon. Then the light turned brighter and greener, and streamers of the light curved and thrashed like a whip, curling back on themselves like ribbons. The waves of pale-green fire washed the sky and I almost thought I could hear the lights swishing, like the rustling of a dress.

It was beautiful, and exciting, and magical. I thought of Lucien's story of the foxes with glistening fur. Well, the foxes were running tonight.

I started to wake Ferris, but something stopped me. I wanted the silence, this night sky now awash with pulsating color, all to myself. I felt drawn up into those glittering stars and northern lights. Ferris was afraid of the dark, but I loved the night.

"You're not afraid of much, are you?" Ferris once asked, but I was. I was afraid of losing what meant the most to me: this land, my roots, my footing in this dark, stony soil. I doubted that anyone had ever felt deeper roots than I felt for my home, the farm and the land. Owen Campbell had, maybe, though he'd left a home across the ocean. How was I going to leave this? If I had to, I felt my life would be over before it even really got started. I was like one of those stars, held in place by invisible strings that when cut would send me spinning, out of control, through the sky until I hit unknown forces and burned up.

I suddenly felt very alone. But I still didn't wake Ferris. It wasn't her cheerful banter I craved. I wanted Grandpa's comforting presence, as warm and solid as homemade bread, and for everything to be the way it used to be. I wanted Father to have two legs, the old barn still standing, and for Grandpa to be alive. Grandpa would have helped me save the farm. Grandpa had given his life to the farm. I knew where I'd gotten my feelings for the farm. "You're like me," Grandpa'd once told me and I'd swelled with pride. He'd never said that to Lucien. Grandpa had loved the dark soil and wide sky. Maybe he was up there somewhere, in those dark spaces between the stars, looking down. I wondered if Grandpa could see me now. I thought about asking him for help to save the farm, but then I thought that maybe that was wrong. You were supposed to talk to God, not someone else as if he were God. And with everything else going on in the world: wars and famine, earthquakes and floods, I didn't think God had time to worry about saving one little farm in northern Vermont. It was all I'd worried about for weeks, but my worrying hadn't helped one whit. In twelve hours, the cows, the machinery, and my life as I knew it would be gone.

I realized sleeping out had been a mistake. The place I really wanted to be this last night was with the cows: Ginger, Clementine, Delilah and the others before they were sold and I'd never see them again.

I took the flashlight to find my way back home and left Ferris sleeping. She'd be mad when she woke up and found I'd left her there alone, but I'd deal with that tomorrow. Besides, it served her right for not backing me up about running away.

Lucien had kept the cows in for the night, bedding them down with fresh sawdust in hopes they'd stay clean before the auction. As I stepped into the stable, I took a deep breath and tears stung my eyes as I realized this would be the last time I would do this. Never again, in this barn, would I smell the warm, yeasty earthiness of cows and hay and manure, teach a calf to drink from a pail, hear the hum of milking machines or the soft rhythms of cows chewing their cuds.

Ginger was lying down in her stanchion and she regarded me with her large brown eyes. I knelt beside her, resting my head on her side, and listened to the steady thump of blood pumping through her heart. Like a new puppy quieted by a ticking clock, the sound calmed me and I fell asleep against her.

Sometime later, I woke to the creak of the barn door opening. I heard the latch click shut and the sound of footsteps in the stable. I held my breath, listening. Blood pounded in my ears and my mind raced.

Who would be sneaking into the barn at this hour? Was someone planning on stealing something? And what would they do to me if they found me here?

Trying not to make a sound, I scuttled backward through the manger and along the wall until I could sneak out through the milk house. Then I ran to the house.

"Cripes, Iris," Lucien said when I shook him awake. "You about gave me a heart attack."

"Hurry! There's somebody in the barn," I said. "I was out there and I heard someone come in."

Lucien slipped on his pants and sneakers and I followed him downstairs.

"Gimme the light," Lucien said as we made our way across the yard to the barn. He was grumpy from being woken in the middle of the night.

"What were you doing out here, anyway?" he wanted to know.

What could I tell him that would sum up my jumble of emotions, that would express my feelings of love for the farm, and of loss?

"Saying good-bye," was what I said.

Lucien put a finger to his lips and I tiptoed behind, wincing as the door creaked open.

Lucien played the flashlight around the stable and we

didn't see anything unusual. He flashed the light along the row of cows.

"Looks like you weren't the only one," Lucien whispered as the glow of the light found Father asleep with his head resting against Delilah.

CHAPTER FOURTEEN

I watched the auction from the attic window and thought I'd choke from the lump in my throat. I hoped nobody would show up, that all our neighbors would stay home so Father would have to keep the cows and equipment. But an hour before the auction was set to begin, the long hill leading up to our place was lined with cars and trucks, bringing the men and women who'd been here only a few months ago to build the barn. It seemed like a slap in the face, to sell after all their effort, but Father said they'd understand. A lot of those same people were wondering how long they'd be able to hold onto their own farms, he said.

Clementine was led out and sold, then Belle and Tess. I could hardly bear to see Ginger sold; I'd always thought of her as my cow. I was glad when Jervis Potter bought her. He was a kind, gentle man; I was sure he'd take good care of her.

I heard footsteps on the stairs.

"I've been looking for you," Lucien said. "Mama's worried about how you're feeling. Why don't you come downstairs? I know it's not easy to watch the auction."

"When do we have to go?" I watched Ed Bolton, a farmer from over Craftsbury way, make a bid on the John Deere tractor. I wondered if the auctioneer had told the bidders it was a balky starter in cold weather. And there was too much play in the steering wheel. But I liked it better than the Farmall. It was the Farmall that had turned over on Grandpa.

"Well," said Lucien, "the new mill will be opening up in another month or so, so probably around November. Mama and Father have to sell this place first."

My hopes lifted. No one around here had money to buy a farm. Maybe it wouldn't sell.

"Probably someone from down-country will buy it for a summer place," Lucien said, and my heart sank. They wouldn't love this place like I did. They wouldn't feel the same way about Beech Hill, wouldn't know when and where to look for the orchids, or trillium, or the blue heron's nest, and would probably dig up Mama's flowers to plant something else.

Lucien was thinking along the same lines.

"I'm going to dig up one of the lilacs for Mama to take to White River Junction," he said, "and the moss rose." Our great-great-great grandmother, Catherine Campbell, Owen's mother, had brought the moss rose over from Scotland when she and William Campbell had immigrated to Vermont ten years after Owen had settled here. It had been in our family ever since.

"It might help that old rose to be moved," Lucien said, looking at me. "Sometimes plants get rootbound and they grow better in new soil."

I thought that a strange thing to say. Was he trying to tell me something? Well, I could tell him I was one plant that would grow best right here on the farm, rootbound and all.

I went downstairs with Lucien. Mama and Aunt Lurdine were sitting at the table. Aunt Lurdine chatted away as usual, but Mama looked almost as sad as I felt.

"Oh, Iris, there you are," Aunt Lurdine purred. "I was just talking about the opportunities that are ahead for you. Won't you be lucky, not having to live on this smelly old farm anymore. White River Junction's not a cultural center by any means, but it's a much better place for a girl to grow up into a young lady."

Even Mama knew Aunt Lurdine had gone too far.

"Now, Lurdine, we're not moving because we want to. There's nothing wrong with growing up on a farm, as you should know. I happen to think it's the best place of all."

The auction finished up before suppertime. The cows were trucked off to other farms, the tractors driven away, and the caravan of cars wound down the hill again. Even though Mama, Father, and Lucien were there with me, the farm felt lonelier than it ever had. Lucien headed out the door once to milk, forgetting for a moment there weren't any cows to milk.

I felt lost, too. Never in all my life, had I not had chores to do. You would have thought that after thirteen years of morning and evening chores, every day, I would have been glad to not have to feed calves, fork hay to the cows, lug pails of milk to the milk house, and scrape manure, but I wasn't. I hated it. The farm wasn't just where I lived, it was who I was, and without it, I wasn't sure who I was anymore.

I took to watching the road for unfamiliar cars. If I saw one, my mouth went dry and my stomach twisted. I felt close to panic thinking it was someone planning to buy the farm. Even with the cows and equipment gone, I still held out hope we wouldn't move, Father would change his mind and buy back the cows and we'd be farming again. I thought if I watched the road, I'd somehow be able to keep people away. I thought it was my secret until I heard Mama talking to Aunt Lurdine.

"I'm worried about Iris," Mama said. "She's been as jumpy as a cat."

"So has Draper," Aunt Lurdine said. "I declare, I don't know what's gotten into that boy. He hasn't seemed right all summer." I knew why, but I couldn't tell.

"Have you found a place in White River Junction yet?" Aunt Lurdine asked.

"Not yet," Mama said. "We have to sell this place first. I wish we could move now, so Iris could start off the new year in her new school, but we just can't."

Ferris and I started back to school in September. I knew I was only going to be there a couple more months, but it was good to see all the familiar faces. Ferris had suggested that instead of running away I should ask Mama if I could live with her family, then I wouldn't have to change schools, and I'd at least be closer to the land I loved, but I was pretty sure Mama wouldn't go along with that idea, either. Besides, as much as I hated to move, I already felt I'd lost too much to give up all my family, too.

Alice was still there, still in the same faded dress and still with her hungry look, but something had changed in me. As I sat watching her, I felt ashamed of how I'd treated her. She looked so alone. I felt sorry for her. I screwed up my courage and asked her to eat lunch with Ferris and me.

From then on, Ferris and I took to picking her for our

teams at recess and she ate lunch with us every day, though she never had much to eat. Some days, all she had for lunch was a mayonnaise sandwich made with stale bread. I took to bringing extra for her, but she was too proud, I guess, 'cause she'd say she was full, though her face always had that pinched, hungry look.

She told us she had five sisters and two brothers, all living with her mother (she didn't mention a father and we didn't ask), but she wouldn't talk about herself. I invited her over to our house several times, but she said she had chores to get home to. She never asked me over, either. She always had some excuse, like she had to take care of her brothers and sisters, or her mom was sick, but the more excuses she made up, the more I figured she was trying to hide something. So one afternoon, without her seeing me, I followed her home.

It was a beautiful afternoon, early in October. All the maples had shed their leaves, and long streamers of geese had been passing overhead for days. Their wild music always twisted my heart; it was the saddest, lonesomest sound I knew, and the one I loved most. The only time I ever had an urge to go someplace was when the wild geese flew overhead, and something in me wanted to go with them.

I followed Alice out to the Sneeze River. Great-great-grandfather Owen had named the river. Father said he must have had hay fever. I was surprised Alice was heading this way; the nearest house was almost a mile away.

The Mitchells were living by the river, but I wasn't prepared for what I saw. I'd expected a run-down house, maybe with tar paper on it, or a trailer even, something she might be ashamed of. But when I peeked through the bushes, my breath caught in my throat. The Mitchells were living in a house of hay.

Hay bales made up the walls, stacks five bales high, and the roof was an old rowboat that some fisherman had abandoned years ago because it leaked. It was just a tiny place, not even as big as the playhouse Father had built me once, and not as well built. I couldn't believe nine people lived in there. With everybody inside, you could have stirred them with a spoon.

While I watched, two kids flew out of the house, one of them beating the other with a stick. A woman followed them. She was almost as thin as Alice and looked as worn-out as an old harness. I couldn't hear anything they said from where I stood, so I watched for a few more minutes, then I ran home. Mama was horrified when I told her.

"That poor woman," she kept saying. "Those poor children. We have to do something."

Mama sent me to my room to get some clothes together for Alice.

"Put in some of your nicer clothes, too, not just the old ones," Mama said, which was fine with me. I hated my dress-up clothes. I put in all three dresses I owned, plus two barrettes and the bra Aunt Lurdine had given me. I'd have thrown in the nylon stockings, too, but I'd hung onions in them when Lucien and I had cleaned out the garden and stored the vegetables in the cellar.

Mama filled a box with clothes that Lucien and I had long outgrown for the younger children, and put in her best Sunday dress, the blue one that Father said brought out the blue in her eyes, for Mrs. Mitchell. Then she fixed an even bigger box of food: flour, sugar, cornmeal, jams, pickles, preserves, and four loaves of her good bread, hot from the oven. She went down cellar to get vegetables to put in the box, and came back up lugging the onions in my nylon stockings. She stared hard at me, and I figured she was going to let me have it, but then she laughed, a beautiful, clear laugh I hadn't heard for months.

She waited until after supper, then asked Lucien to put the boxes in the back of the truck.

"Where you headed?" Father asked.

"Iris and I have some business to do," was all Mama would say.

The moon was shimmering like melted silver on the river when we drove to the Mitchells. Mama turned the engine off when we were still several hundred yards away. Without a word between us, we lugged those heavy boxes to the hay house, trying to make as little noise as possible, and left them a few feet from the doorway. I thought my arms were going to drop off before we got there. I was glad the Mitchells didn't have a dog, too, that would have barked and told them we were there, but I'm sure Mrs. Mitchell had all the mouths to feed she could handle.

Back in the truck, I shivered from the excitement and secrecy. Mama sat for a moment, staring out the window before she started the motor.

"I wish there was more we could do for them," she said.

That was Mama all over. It didn't matter what she was going through, and she'd been through plenty this year, Mama always had time and concern for others in need. And the more I thought about it, the more I realized how being wrapped up in my own sadness had made me selfish, and not thinking of anybody else. I was feeling bad and thought I had a right to be, but Mama did, too, and she was still helping others. It made me see how strong Mama really was, and how I wanted to be more like her, not selfish and self-centered like Aunt Lurdine.

Mama turned to me.

"I'm so sorry for all that's happened, Iris. I don't know what to say to you except I'm sorry. I know how you feel about the farm. I hate to leave it, too."

"Lucien said people are like plants. They have to move every so often to keep from being rootbound."

Even in the darkness, I could feel Mama smiling to herself.

"Any plant wants a permanent home someday," she said. "A maple tree can't grow to its full size unless it stays in one place, sending its roots down deeper, year after year. Your roots are deep, Iris. And so are Lucien's. He just doesn't know it yet."

CHAPTER FIFTEEN

For me, that night trip to the Mitchells seemed like just a beginning. I kept wondering how I could help Alice more. That is what we should have been doing in that stupid 4-H group, trying to do something for someone who needed our help. I thought about asking folks for money to help her, but I knew right off that was out of the question. Mama would be horrified if I went to begging, even if it was for somebody else.

It was an unwritten code in the Northeast Kingdom that even if you were starving you didn't ask for help. If help came, that was one thing. But you didn't ask for it. In fact, dying was considered preferable to the disgrace of begging or accepting welfare. You didn't pry into anybody else's business, either, but if you knew somebody was in trouble, you did what you could to help them. You had to be careful doing it, though. You couldn't go right up to someone and hand them money, or food, or clothes. That was why we'd left the boxes at Mrs. Mitchell's under cover of darkness.

I wasn't even allowed to go trick-or-treating. Mama, along with the rest of the church families, likened it to begging, so instead, all the kids in the church collected money for

UNICEF. I never knew exactly where the money went, other than it helped feed and clothe starving children.

It was Mama's boxes to the Mitchells, and Halloween coming, that gave me the idea to help Alice. If I was going to be collecting money for someone, it might as well be for someone I knew and cared about. And I knew one person I could get to help me. Draper.

Draper didn't want to help, but he wasn't about to say no to me, seeing as how I was keeping his secret about the fire. Still, he grumbled.

"Just about everybody in Gilead is poor. Why don't we go someplace we've never gone before, like Greensboro? They've got more money over there."

I thought he had a good idea, but seeing as how Mama always drove us around on Halloween night to collect for UNICEF, I didn't see how we could get to Greensboro without her knowing about it.

But on Halloween night, after we'd gone to all the houses in Gilead and there was still a lot of empty space in my UNICEF can, I figured I'd give his idea a try.

"Why don't we drive over to Greensboro and collect money there," I ventured. "I bet we could get lots more over there."

Mama looked doubtful. We'd never gone anywhere to collect but right around Gilead.

"Doesn't seem right for us to go and bother folks over thataway."

"It's for a good cause, Aunt Edith," Draper said.

There was still doubt in Mama's eyes, but I was sure she was picturing the Mitchell children and their hay-bale house in her mind. She drove us to Greensboro, and we knocked on doors till after nine o'clock. Even Mama admitted that the trip had been worth it; Draper and I'd collected $39.33 which was about thirty dollars more than we usually collected. We'd never seen so much money and I was crowing inside thinking of how much Mrs. Mitchell would be able to buy for Alice and her brothers and sisters.

Only trouble was, I hadn't completely thought out my plan. I never figured on Mama mentioning to Aunt Lurdine about our success. Mama never bragged on her children, but I think she'd been feeling pretty good, too, at the money that would go to needy children. Anyway, two days after Halloween, Aunt Lurdine came flying into the yard, her eyes flashing sparks.

"I never thought I'd live to see the day when someone in my own family took to stealing," Aunt Lurdine said. Her voice shook.

Mama was aghast.

"Who are you talking about, sister?"

"Iris," Aunt Lurdine said. "She never handed in her UNICEF money. She stole it."

I thought Mama had stopped breathing. I was wishing I could melt into the ground, be anywhere other than where I was, before Mama turned to me with fire in her eyes and sorrow in her heart, and I'd have to explain what had happened. But Mama never looked at me.

"Iris does not steal," Mama said firmly.

"But she didn't hand in . . ."

"Did Draper hand in his money?" Mama interrupted.

"You leave Draper out of this," Aunt Lurdine screeched. "Draper's a good boy. He wouldn't have done this if Iris hadn't put him up to it."

Oh, I wanted to scream at her, to tell her that her precious little boy wasn't so perfect after all.

"Lurdine," Mama said. "Iris does not steal. I think you had better go home now."

The only person more surprised than Aunt Lurdine herself was me. Mama had never talked to Aunt Lurdine that way.

The color drained from Aunt Lurdine's face. I think she was going to say something, but one look at Mama's face and she turned in a huff. Mama waited until Aunt Lurdine had driven off before she turned to me.

"You took it for Alice, didn't you," Mama said. It wasn't a question, and I nodded. I figured she was going to chew me out now.

"I can't think of a better use for that money," Mama said. "I wish you'd told me what you meant to do, so we could have told Reverend Mackenzie what you wanted to do with the collection. I'm sure he would have approved."

"I haven't given it to the Mitchells yet," I said. "I thought I'd have to leave it at night again."

"Well, then, let's go see Reverend Mackenzie now," Mama said. "Go get your coat. It's cold out."

As we drove into town, I held the UNICEF can tightly in my lap. For the first mile, Mama didn't say anything. I wondered if down deep, maybe she was mad at me. Then I heard her giggle.

"I expect Lurdine is right put out with me," she said.

I laughed, too. I imagined she was, too, and I can't say I was sorry that Mama had stood up to Aunt Lurdine. It seemed, sometimes, that Mama was always doing things to embarrass me, like tying my milk money up in a hankie, like I was still five years old, or if I had a sore throat, sending me to school with an old sock full of liniment tied around my neck, but sometimes she did something that really made me proud of her, and at that moment, I only knew how proud I was of Mama.

Reverend Mackenzie thought it a fine idea to give the money to the Mitchells. He even suggested that we take up a collection on Sunday for them, and Mama and I went home feeling pretty pleased with ourselves.

Mama was cooking supper when I carried the grain sack in and dumped all the supplies on the table.

"What's all this?" Mama asked. Then she looked more closely.

"My frying pan!" she exclaimed. "And my spatula. I was wondering where there'd gone. Where'd you find them?"

"I had them, Mama," I said. "I hid them up by the old cellar-hole."

"Why?" Mama asked.

"Because I wasn't going to move to White River Junction with you," I said slowly. "I was going to run away and live in the woods."

I expected Mama to yell at me and tell me I was being ridiculous and childish, but sometimes Mama surprised me.

"What changed your mind?" she asked gently.

"Alice," I said. "She doesn't have a house to live in, or much food to eat. I've never had to go hungry, or sleep under a boat. I love this farm, but it wouldn't be home anymore without you and Father and Lucien."

Mama hugged me.

"Oh, Iris," she said. "I'm sorry this is so hard for you. I don't want to leave, either. I'm going to miss this place, too, but a family needs to stick together."

I thought of how lucky I was to have Mama for my mother and not Aunt Lurdine. Mama should have taught the 4-H group; she would have had us doing things for the betterment of the community instead of stupid things like growing fingernails. She might have even figured out a way to help the Mitchells, get them a better place to live. I was sure the people in our town would have helped; look how they had worked together to build us a new barn.

The idea came to me with stunning clarity, an idea so startling yet so simple I couldn't believe I hadn't thought of it sooner.

"Mama, couldn't we do for Alice's family what our neighbors did for us? Couldn't we build them a house to live in?"

CHAPTER SIXTEEN

Mama was delighted with the idea, and she went right to work talking to the neighbors. By Sunday, there was a plan underfoot to hold a house-raising for the Mitchells. Nothing fancy, mind you, but a place with four walls and a roof, a lot more than they had now.

Mama and I were both excited about it. It was something hopeful and kept our thoughts off our own troubles. After church, Mama met with a group to talk about the house-raising. Olin Marckres asked about wood for the project, and the group fell silent. Uncle Sturgis had supplied the lumber for our barn, but he couldn't be asked again, and with everyone busy cutting corn and getting it into silos, there just wasn't time to be cutting timber for a house. Then it came to me.

"Mama," I said, tugging her sleeve. "There's all them logs up in our woods that Father and Lucien cut."

Mama's face lit up. "Oh, Iris, what a wonderful thought. That's settled then. We've got the wood."

After a little more discussion, Noel Piette said he'd saw the logs up for free if someone could haul them to his sawmill, and Hilas Bumps said his two middle sons could handle that. So it all seemed settled, and Mama and I went home feeling like Christmas had come and we were keeping a wonderful secret. I think Mama felt especially proud to be supplying the lumber for the project after the neighbors had put up our barn for us, and I felt I was making a trade. If I had to lose my own house, at least I could leave Gilead knowing I'd helped Alice to have a real home of her own.

The lumber was ready a week later, and the date for the house-raising was set for the middle of November. I felt like an old hand at raisings now, after our barn, and I wanted to help with the hammering and sawing. Mama looked doubtful, thinking I ought to be helping the women with the meal, but Father broke in to say I could help by running and fetching things for the men, as long as I didn't get in the way. That wasn't the help I'd had in mind, but it was still better than helping fix the dinner, so I didn't put up a fuss. And it pleased me to see Father involved in the project; it was the first interest he'd shown in anything since his accident.

Father, Mama, and I were in the front car as we all pulled into the Mitchells' yard early Saturday morning. For the longest while, we just sat and stared, not saying anything.

The Mitchells had left. The rowboat was on the ground, on its side, and one wall of the bales had tipped over. There were two or three old cooking pots scattered around the yard, and pieces of a kitchen chair, but other than that, there was no sign of life, no sign that anyone had ever lived there.

Mama kept apologizing to our neighbors there, taking the blame when I knew it wasn't her fault. It had been my idea and it'd turned out to be a bad one. Why was it every idea I'd had all summer had backfired: running away, selling raspberries, and now building this house? Mama was protecting me, but our neighbors didn't blame her.

"That's all right, Edith. You didn't know they was fixing to move on," but I knew how Mama felt. I was angry at Mrs. Mitchell, angry at Alice. She hadn't been in school the last couple of days, but Alice missed a lot of school, taking care of her brothers and sisters, so I hadn't thought anything of it. Why hadn't she told me they were leaving? She hadn't even left a note. It was as if I hadn't even existed for her, and I felt betrayed. I'd wanted to have a part in doing something really nice for her, to leave knowing she had four warm walls around her before winter set in. If only they'd stayed one more day. We'd have gotten the house up and then they could have stayed for good.

"Maybe the house would have driven them off," Mama said, mostly to herself.

That sounded crazy to me. Why would a new house do that?

"I think she might have felt she owed us too much," Mama said, "It's hard to live with folks you feel beholden to." Mama sighed.

"Well, I guess we might as well go home," she said.

"No," Father piped up and we all turned to look at him. "Let's go ahead and build the house anyway."

"But why?" Mama said. "The Mitchells are gone."

The words leaped out of my mouth before Father could speak.

"Because someone else will come along who needs it," I said, and Father nodded, a half-smile on his lips.

Not one person in the group disagreed, and so we worked all day, friends and neighbors, no longer building a house for the Mitchells but for someone we hadn't even met yet, and by dusk, a small house stood on the bank of the Sneeze River.

We all stood to admire our work and Mama shook her head.

"That poor woman," she said softly. "I wish she'd stayed. She could have made a home here for those children."

We were quiet as we rode home. I longed for supper and a hot bath, and I was bone-tired, but it was a good tired, the feeling you get when you've worked hard and done something for someone else.

"I'm proud of you, Iris," Mama said quietly. "That was a wonderful idea," and my heart sang.

Our headlights caught Uncle Sturgis sitting on our porch steps waiting for us. He'd left the house-raising before us, to go home.

"Sturgis!" Mama said, stepping from the car. "Is there something wrong?"

Uncle Sturgis nodded.

"Draper's gone," he said. "He's been missing since this morning. I thought he was home with Lurdine, and she thought he was with me at the house-raising. Lurdine's afraid he's been kidnapped."

"What?" Mama said, and Father held up his hand.

"Hold on," he said. "I'm sure that's not the case. You know how Lurdine gets worked up. He may have just run away for a few hours. Most kids do that at one time or another."

Uncle Sturgis nodded.

"I thought of that, too, but I called some of his friends and no one seems to know where he is." Uncle Sturgis twisted his hat in his hands.

"Something's been bothering that boy all summer, the way he's been so jumpy, won't look you straight in the face and he's troubled by nightmares almost every night. He just picks at his food, too. I didn't pay too much attention, figured it couldn't be anything serious. Now I have a feeling it was."

"Edith," he said to Mama, "I know you're tired, but I'd be mighty obliged if you'd come be with Lurdine. She's frantic with worry and everything I say makes her worse."

"Of course, Sturgis," Mama said. "Let me just grab my coat."

My mind had been racing. I didn't know where Draper was hiding, but I was pretty sure he had run away. And I was even surer I knew why. This had gone on long enough. How Aunt Lurdine felt didn't concern me much; she could just keel over with worry for all I cared, but I could see how worried Uncle Sturgis was. It was time I said something. I hadn't been able to help Alice, but maybe I could help Draper, though more'n likely he wouldn't see it that way.

I took a deep breath.

"Uncle Sturgis, I got something to tell you."

CHAPTER SEVENTEEN

I stunned them all, telling them about Draper, but I guess it hit Uncle Sturgis hardest, it being his son that had caused so much trouble. I felt bad about hurting Uncle Sturgis, and wished I could have told Aunt Lurdine instead. I wanted to see her face when she found out what her precious boy had done.

Uncle Sturgis stood silent, thinking things through in his mind, then turned toward Father.

"We can never make this up to you, Hazen," he said.

"There's nothing to make up," Father said. "I don't blame the boy."

I couldn't believe Father would say that. Draper *was* to blame.

Uncle Sturgis answered like he'd read my mind.

"If it weren't for him, you wouldn't have had your accident."

"I got myself trapped under that tree," Father said. "Not Draper. Let's just concentrate on finding him." He went into the house to gather up flashlights, and Uncle Sturgis followed him.

"They won't do a thing to him," I said bitterly. "He

burned our barn, and made Father lose his leg, and now Father's acting like Draper never did anything wrong."

Mama studied me.

"If your father can forgive Draper, why can't you?" she asked quietly and I didn't have an answer.

We looked for Draper all night. Uncle Sturgis called home from Ora White's to tell Aunt Lurdine the reason behind Draper's disappearance (I didn't suppose she had taken the news well) and Ora White, hearing that Draper was lost, had made calls of his own to round up searchers. As word spread, neighbors arrived in the darkness, offering to help, the same neighbors that had helped build the house just that day and had gone home in the evening to do their own chores. I knew they were all tired, just as we were, but not a one complained and they all just pitched in to find Draper. After all that had happened this summer, I was beginning to understand the blessing of good neighbors.

We split up into groups so we could cover as much of the town and surrounding hills as possible. Lucien and I took the ridge and Beech Hill. We walked for hours, shining our flashlights and calling until we were hoarse.

As I trudged along behind Lucien, my feet dragging from exhaustion, my rage toward Draper ran white-hot until I thought my head would explode. Here he had everybody worried about him, thinking "Oh, that poor boy" when he was only hiding because he was too cowardly to own up to what he'd done. I hoped he had run away, so far he wouldn't come home again and I wouldn't be reminded every time I looked at him how he'd destroyed everything I held dear.

At daybreak, we gathered at our farmhouse. Mama came home to help feed the searchers but Father surprised us all by handing out sandwiches and cups of hot coffee he'd made. I hadn't known Father even knew how to turn on the stove, but not being able to search with us, he'd done what he could to help. He spoke to the group as they ate.

"I know you all have milking to do. Go home, get your chores done, and then we'll meet back here."

As folks headed home, Father pulled Mama aside. He spoke low but I made out what he said.

"I walked over to Ora's and called the sheriff. He's going to bring a search dog with him." Father lowered his voice even further and I had to strain to hear him.

"Don't say a word to Lurdine, but he's going to bring dredging equipment to drag the river."

Until then, I hadn't been worried. I was sure Draper had run away and I knew why. But those words chilled my blood. The sheriff was going to drag the river for Draper's body, and for the first time, I had doubts that Draper was safe. Was it possible someone could have kidnapped him? We heard about such things happening in other places. Or was it possible Draper was so upset over burning down the barn and being responsible for Father getting hurt that he'd think of suicide? Would he have gone to the river?

I realized Uncle Sturgis was talking to me.

"Draper spends a lot of time with you," he said. "Where would he go, Iris?"

I shook the doubts from my mind so I could concentrate. During the night, I'd been so angry I'd only thought of how I hated Draper. Now I needed to think like him. I racked my brain, trying to remember all the places we'd played to-gether, but Lucien and I had already checked those places during the night. I thought of the places Grandpa had taken Draper and me and the place he'd promised to take us but never had.

The place he'd told us about but had died before he could show us.

I blinked and stared at Uncle Sturgis.

"The cave," I squeaked.

Uncle Sturgis only looked puzzled.

"Cave?" Father asked. "You mean that old cave on the back side of Beech Hill?" I nodded.

"I hope to God he didn't go there," Father said. "Why, that's a bear den."

Probably that bear that had startled me while I was picking raspberries, I thought. If Draper had found that cave and crawled in, it didn't take a genius to figure out that bear wouldn't take kindly to finding him in there.

A mixture of fear and guilt formed a cold, hard knot in my stomach. Mama sometimes said, "Be careful what you wish for, it might come true," and for the first time I understood what she meant. I'd wanted Draper to be punished. I'd wished for something bad to happen to him. But now that it looked like something had, I realized I hadn't wanted that at all.

"Guess we best be getting up there," Uncle Sturgis said. "If there's trouble around, that boy's sure to find it."

"You know where this cave is?" he asked me.

I shook my head.

"Grandpa never showed us."

"I know where it is," Father said.

"You can't go up there, Hazen," Mama said. "Just tell Sturgis and Lucien where it is, and they'll go."

"That cave's stayed a secret so long because it's so well hidden," Father said. "Besides, you've been telling me since I got home I need to get out and get used to this new leg." He looked from Lucien to Uncle Sturgis.

"Ready when you are," he said, and I scrambled to my feet.

"Hold on," Mama said, placing a hand on my shoulder. "You're not going anywhere except to bed."

As tired as I was, I couldn't bear the thought of missing out on this adventure.

"I thought of the cave," I said, glaring at Mama. "I should be able to go with them," but Mama wouldn't budge. I looked pleadingly at Lucien, hoping he'd back me up, but Father spoke first.

"She's right, Iris. You've been up all night."

And so I watched them go off without me.

"I know you're angry with me," Mama said, "but I don't want you in danger, too."

"I guess I'll go to bed now," I said, yawning and stretching, but I didn't fool Mama one bit.

"You'd better just sit with me for a while," she said. "Knowing you, you'd probably sneak out your window and go off to join them," which was exactly what I'd had in mind.

We heard the whine of a car engine and Mama shaded her eyes to see who was coming.

A dark green car pulled into the yard and Aunt Lurdine tumbled out. She looked awful, her hair all wild and her eyes red and swollen.

"Oh, Edith, I can't bear it!" she wailed, falling into Mama's arms. "Something's happened to him, I just know it!"

Mama patted her on the back.

"Now, now, you don't know that," she soothed. "I'm sure he's all right. Iris had an idea where he might be hiding, in a cave Papa told them about, and the men have gone there.

I'll just bet they're going to be back soon with him, safe and sound."

At the mention of my name, Aunt Lurdine had stopped listening and swiveled her head to hunt me down.

"Sturgis told me what she said," she sputtered, shaking a finger at me. "I can't believe Iris is spreading such lies. If you don't punish her, I will. I should never have let Draper spend time with her. She's a bad influence."

"That's enough, Lurdine," Mama said quietly. "I know you're upset, but I won't have you speaking that way to Iris. As for punishment, it's Draper that should have been disciplined a long time ago. You've spoiled and coddled him."

"And you've let Iris grow up wild and headstrong," Aunt Lurdine screeched. "She should act more like a lady."

"No," said Mama. "She shouldn't. I like Iris just the way she is. In the most difficult year of her life, she's shown kindness and courage and unselfishness, and I've never been prouder of anyone in my whole life." Her voice quavered and I thought she was going to cry. And for a moment, I thought I would, too.

"Iris, I think it'd be best if you went to your room now and tried to get some sleep," Mama said, her eyes pleading for me to mind her without arguing, for once. And for once, I did.

I meant to stay in my room for only a few minutes, enough time for Mama to direct her attention back on Aunt Lurdine and away from me, and I would sneak out to join Father, Lucien, and Uncle Sturgis, but I made the mistake of closing my eyes and I was asleep when they brought Draper home.

Chapter Eighteen

Aunt Lurdine screamed and hustled Draper off to the hospital, even though he wasn't hurt, before I had a chance to see him, but Father and Lucien took turns filling me in on the details of the great adventure I'd missed.

As it turned out, Draper had stumbled onto the cave and crawled in to spend the night. The cave was unoccupied at the time, but only, Father supposed, because bears are nocturnal and mostly feed at night. The bear had returned in the morning, intending to spend the day undisturbed, sleeping. Draper had heard something approaching and as the bear stuck its head into the cave, Draper had screamed, and whacked the bear on the nose with a stick. The bear yelped (probably more from surprise than pain, Lucien guessed) and backed out so quickly it lost its footing and tumbled down the steep slope. That's when Father and Uncle Sturgis and Lucien had looked up to see a bear rolling their way. Lucien and Uncle Sturgis had leaped out of the way, but Father, hampered by his artificial leg, wasn't able to move so fast. The bear came to a stop and got up, disoriented, and headed right for Father. Father tore off his new leg and brandished it over his head, yelling like a troop of rebel soldiers, but the bear was so close he didn't have time to swerve and he ran over Father.

At this, Mama and I both gasped and Father nodded.

"Yup, bowled me right over," he said, his eyes glittering with excitement.

"I was afraid to shoot," Lucien added, "for fear I'd hit Father."

Father continued, "That bear wasn't out to hurt me, he was just trying to get away, and he kept running till he was out of sight."

Father pulled off his leg and held it up to show us.

"One of the rods is bent a little, but it still works all right. I don't suppose it's insured against bear damage."

"Dear Lord, Hazen," Mama breathed, her face white. "You could have been killed. I should never have let you go up there."

"Edith, dear," Father said, pulling her close, "I wouldn't have missed that for the world." He almost smiled. "I imagine that bear doesn't want to see another human for a long time."

Once Mama had calmed down, she said she'd take me over to visit Draper. She insisted he'd be glad to see me.

I was sure I was the last person Draper wanted to see, and I wasn't too eager to face him, either, but I have to admit my heart softened somewhat when I saw him and realized how easily that bear could have killed him.

"You told Dad," were the first words out of Draper's mouth.

"Yes, I did," I said simply. I wondered if Draper was waiting for me to apologize for squealing on him, but he'd be waiting a long time, after what he did.

Draper didn't say anything for a few moments.

"I'm glad you did," he said finally. "I feel better now. I'm still real sorry for what I did, but now I don't have to hide it anymore," and the last of my bitterness toward him melted away.

"I guess I'm just a big chicken," Draper said.

I sat on the bed next to him.

"Whacking a bear with a stick is about the bravest thing I ever heard," I said, wanting to be generous. "I wish I'd been there. I got stuck back here with Mama and your mom."

"What'd she say?" Draper asked, meaning Aunt Lurdine.

"She was pretty mad," I said. "Mostly at me. But Mama stood up to her."

Draper considered what I'd said.

"I think I'd rather face that bear again," he said, seriously, and I fell over laughing, delighted with the image of Mama whacking Aunt Lurdine on the nose with a stick.

With Draper safe, and the weight of the secret off my shoulders, and Father improving, things would have been great except for the fact that we were still going to move and nothing had changed that. Father had come across the business card the New York man had given him back in the spring, had given him a call, and the man and his wife were driving up in a week or so to make arrangements to buy the farm. As the days wound down, getting closer to that inevitability, so did my spirits until they matched perfectly with the dreariness of November.

November had always been my least favorite month, a wet, gray season caught between the colors of fall and the stark, cold beauty of winter, a month that seemed to have no beauty of its own. What I hated most was deer season, when hordes of hunters descended on the Northeast Kingdom like a plague of grasshoppers, and gunshots echoed from hill to hill, and the roadsides were littered with beer bottles.

I wasn't allowed to wander in the woods for those two weeks, so I walked all over the farm every day of that last week before deer season started. I felt my time was running out, and I tried to soak up as much of the sights and sounds and smells as I could, to carry with me when I went to White River Junction. I was afraid the same thing would happen to my memories of the farm that happened to my memories of Grandpa, that after a little while I wouldn't remember exactly what Beech Hill looked like, or the exact spots wild ginger and Dutchman's-breeches grew, or where Ginger used to hide her calves up by the old cellar-hole.

I felt as sad and empty as an old grain sack. All along, I'd held out hope that something would happen, Lucien would stay and he and I'd run the farm, just like we had this summer. But deep down, I knew that wouldn't happen.

The trees dripped rain, shrouded in fog, and seemed as pale and lifeless as ghosts, but they weren't lifeless at all. Their energy was stored deep inside to weather the cold winter. Next spring, when the warm sun touched them, the trees would send out their pale green leaves and the cycle of the seasons would keep going like it had always gone, rolling on like a wheel, forever and ever. But I wouldn't be here to see it.

Thinking of spring made me wonder again: how did it keep happening, year after year? Sometimes it came early and sometimes it came late, but it always came, and so much happened all at once when spring came that I wondered how God had ever made it all fit together, so that the grass and trees and flowers all came out at the right time, and the animals lived and raised their families where they were supposed to, and the stars were where they were supposed to be. No one could think of all those things, and make them happen right, year after year. There were a lot of details to being God.

The more I thought of it, the more I wondered. Had God ever made mistakes? When he first made the earth, before there were people around to notice, had he ever done something like put the leaves on trees in the winter, and when the trees died, said Whoops! and tried something different the next year? By the time people were on the earth, God probably had everything figured out, and that's why everything seemed to fit together so well.

The rain stopped, finally, and Friday was clear and cold.

"Thought I'd walk up the hill," Lucien said, when I'd gotten home from school, "and take a look around." He didn't say for the last time, but I could tell he was thinking it. "Wanna come along?"

I was too warm climbing the hill, but standing on top with the wind slicing across the valley from the Green Mountains, I was glad I'd worn my heavy coat. The tops of Mt. Mansfield and Jay Peak were bright with snow, and I knew the last warmth of the year was gone. Winter was speeding down out of Canada, bearing down on us like a freight train.

I felt cold inside, too. We'd be moving soon. Mama had been packing for days, and Uncle Sturgis had come over twice during the week, and he and Father had holed up in the back room, talking about Father's job, most likely. I was just waiting now for the ax to fall.

I heard them before I saw them, a ragged streamer of geese winging south, honking their sad song. Sunlight glinted off their white bodies. Snow geese. I pointed them out to Lucien.

"That's a late flock," Lucien said. "They could've been caught by a storm."

"Maybe they didn't want to go," I said softly. If I were a goose, I'd stay up north as long as I could.

Lucien looked at me.

"They have to leave, Iris. They love it here, but they have to leave, for a little while before they come back. You can do that, too. When you're on your own, you can come back here, even live here again, if you want."

I knew I'd come back, too, when I was old enough, but it seemed like a million years away, and by then, everything would be changed.

"Nobody worked harder than you did this summer," Lucien said. "I'm real proud of you."

If the President himself had given me an award, I wouldn't have been as pleased as I was of Lucien's praise. But I still felt hollow inside, knowing all that work, and all my hope, had been for nothing.

"I'm sorry I've disappointed you," Lucien said. "I'm sorry things couldn't be the way you wanted. None of this is the way any of us wanted."

I felt like weeping, like I'd had enough loss and heartache this summer to last a lifetime, but I didn't cry. There was too much hurt for tears to come now.

"I've been thinking what you said to me when I was going to run away," Lucien said. "I was so mad that you'd over-heard me talking to Telfer and I threatened you if you told anyone. You remember what you said?"

I nodded, too full of emotion to speak. I did remember, but I'd have bet money that Lucien didn't.

"You said, 'You can hit me as much as you want if you just won't run away.' I'll never forget it. I thought I was going to embarrass myself and cry right in front of you.

"You know, Iris," Lucien went on, "it'll be hard at first. But after awhile, you won't miss this place so much."

Oh, you're wrong, Lucien, I thought. As long as I live and even after, as long as there are mountains, and rivers, and stars in the sky, I'll miss this farm with all my heart.

We got back home just as it was turning dark. We were about to sit down to supper when Father asked Lucien if the two of them could talk alone. Lucien was surprised and so was I. What could they have to talk about?

Mama smiled, tiredly.

"We've got to be strong through this move, Iris. For your father. Have you noticed he's seemed a little happier the last few days? I think he's looking forward to this new job at the furniture mill. It'll give him a purpose."

When Father and Lucien came back out, Lucien was smiling.

"We've decided," he said, happily. "I'm going back to school. I've pretty much missed this semester, but I'll drive down there tomorrow and register for classes starting in January."

I tried to be happy for him. No sense in all of us having our hopes and dreams dashed. Lucien would be a good writer, too.

As I headed to bed, Lucien put his hand on my shoulder.

"Things are going to turn out all right," he said. "I can't tell you how I know, but I know."

Aunt Lurdine and Uncle Sturgis came next morning to see Lucien off. We all followed him to the yard, said our good-byes and then the grown-ups filtered back into the house. I was the only one who stayed, trying to hang on to the moment, trying to hang on to our last year on the farm together, just a little while longer. Things would never be the same again, after today.

I watched Lucien drive off, and I felt as hollow as a gourd. All our hard work of the summer had been for nothing. We hadn't saved the farm, and it was time to face up to the fact that we had to move.

I didn't want to be with anyone. I could feel the tears coming on, and I wasn't sure once they started if they'd ever stop, so I sneaked up the stairs, but Father called to me.

"Come down here, Iris," he said, meaning the living room. "We have some things to talk about."

Every one was sitting except Father. He wasn't as self-conscious about his leg anymore, and he was getting around better, even climbing stairs, and going out to the barn though there weren't any chores to do.

Right now, he had the look of a boy with a fistful of pennies in a candy store. Even Mama noticed it.

"Hazen, what's gotten into you?"

Father smiled and I realized it was the first time I'd seen him smile since before the barn burned. I'd forgotten what his smile looked like.

"Shall I tell them, or you, Sturgis?" Father said.

"You go ahead," Uncle Sturgis said. I thought he looked uneasy, like he'd been caught doing something he shouldn't have.

"Oh, Hazen, you're just teasing us," Mama said. "What is it?"

Father stood up straight.

"Sturgis is leaving the company," he said. "He's gonna let Walter take over."

It was obvious Aunt Lurdine hadn't heard this before. Her head shot up like one of those fake ducks in a carnival shoot. I was pretty quick to figure out why Uncle Sturgis hadn't told her. She would have raged at him for days, weakening him until he gave in. This way, announcing it in front of everybody would make it easier to stand his ground.

"Sturgis is going to help us out here," Father continued. "He bought back the cows and most of the equipment sold at the auction. Then he came to talk to me. I think we have a good plan to run this farm together."

I felt like Daniel in the lion's den, thrown to the lions, expecting to be torn to bits and eaten, and then, by the grace of God, coming out without a scratch.

None of us thought we'd heard Father right. Especially Aunt Lurdine. Her mouth opened and closed, no sound coming out, like a fish gasping for air, then it clicked shut like a snap purse. Her eyes looked wild like a caged animal, and if looks could kill, Uncle Sturgis would have been gutted and hanging from the deer tree out front.

Uncle Sturgis looked more comfortable now that the news was out, and was even smiling.

"Yessir," Father said, clearly enjoying his little production. "Sturgis said he's always wanted to be a farmer, but things got in his way." He shot a glance at Aunt Lurdine whose eyes were too glazed to notice much of anything. She looked like she was going to cry and I almost felt sorry for her. Almost.

Aunt Lurdine spun on Uncle Sturgis.

"Have you lost your mind?" she screeched.

"Nope," said Uncle Sturgis, smiling at Father. "I just found it."

Chapter Nineteen

Christmas Day dawned clear and so cold my nose tingled when I stuck it out from under the covers. I ran into Lucien's room and jumped on him, pummeling him awake.

The night before, Father had told us to sleep late in the morning, he'd do the chores for us, but now I was worried.

"Shouldn't we go out and help him?" I asked Lucien. Lucien shook his head.

"No, Iris," he said. "Let him do this alone. He needs to do it, to prove something to himself," and I knew Lucien was right because when Father came in later, he carried about him a sense of quiet satisfaction.

We settled down to Mama's Christmas breakfast of hot graham rolls and maple syrup and applesauce she'd canned in the fall; Mama had always tried to get some food into us on Christmas morning before we opened our gifts. When Lucien and I were children, that had been a difficult task, but we weren't little kids anymore, unable to wait for our presents. Still, Christmas mornings filled me with excitement.

Breakfast finished, we gathered round the tree, a balsam fir Lucien and I'd found on the ridge, and it filled the living room with its resiny fragrance.

Lucien gave me two books: one on birds and the other on astronomy.

"So you can keep learning about both," he said, and he seemed happy with my gift to him, a set of pens and three empty notebooks.

"For you to fill with stories," I said and smiled at him, forgiving him for wanting to escape the farm, and wishing him success as a writer.

We were all talking and laughing, but Lucien fell silent when he opened his gift from Father and Mama. They'd given him a typewriter.

Lucien touched the keys lightly and raised his eyes to Father. They stared at each other, Lucien with a look of wonder on his face and Father with a half-smile on his, and neither of them said a word, but I knew that the tension between them had been laid to rest for good.

All the presents had been opened and I hadn't gotten anything from Mama and Father. I couldn't believe they'd forgotten me, but then, maybe they couldn't afford to get me anything, what with Father's hospital bills and getting Lucien that typewriter. But it didn't really matter. We had the farm back and Father was well again. I had everything I needed.

Father leaned forward and gave my hair a gentle tug.

"You didn't think we'd forgotten you, did you?" he asked. "I believe if you poke your head into Grandpa's room, you'll find your present."

I hadn't been in Grandpa's room since he'd died and I

opened the door cautiously, not wanting to dredge up all my memories of Grandpa but curious to see what Father could have hidden in there.

When I didn't move or say anything, Mama peered around me to see what I was staring at. She gasped.

Two small brown calves lay curled on the braided rug. They looked as delicate and beautiful as fawns.

"You put calves in Dad's room?" Mama said, horrified, and then she began to laugh.

"Oh, Hazen, you're a wonder," she said.

Father was grinning like the Cheshire cat.

"Sturgis and I've had the word out for weeks all around the county that if anyone's cow had twin calves they were to call us. It looked like we were going to end up getting you just one calf and then a fellow from Newport Center called yesterday and Sturgis drove over to pick them up."

I hugged him without speaking and knelt beside the calves so I could stroke their soft hair. The memory of my birthday calves filled my mind, and when one of the calves began to suck on my fingers, I felt tears well up in my eyes.

"In two years, they'll have calves of their own and start giving milk," Father said. "And they'll *still* be good milk producers by the time you graduate college and take over the farm."

I was so busy petting the calves that at first it didn't sink in what he'd said. When it did, I looked up to see my parents with their arms around each other. Father was smiling at me, and his smile kept widening until I felt enveloped in it, and the heat and the love in his eyes washed over me like a wave. I wondered if I'd ever feel this happy again, and I knew that, in years to come, I would look back and remember this as the best Christmas ever. And it wouldn't be only for the calves, or for getting the farm back, or for Father being well again. It would be for what Grandpa, Father, Mama, and Lucien, too, had given me and what I would carry with me all the years of my life—their legacy of love and courage and hope for the future—the gift I would treasure most.